T0068171

SAVING
YESTERDAY

SAVING YESTERDAY

E. THORNTON GOODE, JR.

SAVING YESTERDAY

iUniverse books may be ordered through booksellers or by contacting:

iUniverse
1663 Liberty Drive
Bloomington, IN 47403
www.iuniverse.com
844-349-9409

ISBN: 978-1-6632-5790-1 (sc)
ISBN: 978-1-6632-5789-5 (e)

Library of Congress Control Number: 2023921586

Print information available on the last page.

iUniverse rev. date: 11/22/2023

DEDICATION AND APPRECIATION

This story is dedicated to my wonderful friends, companions and all those I have cared for and loved over the years who are now gone from this life, especially Tristram Coffin, Phillip McDonald, Danny Glass and Julian Green. I could sit here and name so many others but it would be a long list and you'd have no idea who they were. I remember them and that's what is important. Periodically, something will happen, triggering a distant memory of one or several of them. I miss them all.

During the AIDS crisis, I would write on the quilts of those friends who had died. This is what I would say, 'We are immortal as long as we live in the hearts and minds of others. Especially, the hearts and minds of those who love us.'

I must include my mother and father, Marilyn and Gene, who were always great support throughout my entire life. Then, of course, there is my 10th and 11th grade English teacher, Mrs. Bettie Brakebill. Without her incredible support and recommendation, I would never have even considered publication. She is the one who told me that my work needed to be in print.

By including pictures of friends, family and those dear to me in appreciation and representing certain characters in the stories, I have not only kept them immortal in my own heart and mind but in the archives of the copyright offices. As long as copies of my novels remain in the national copyright archives, their pictures will be there for many years to come. It is my way of........ Saving Yesterday.

In this story, I've tried to express what the meaning of love is to me. It's not something you can weigh or put in a box. Often words cannot explain it. But I do believe it's the most valuable thing we can ever have in our lives.

———⚬⚬⚬———

My thanks to Charles Test of Chuck's Toy Land for the use of the picture of the 1914, 4-48 Packard, so the reader can see what a wonderful car it was. You will see it later as you read the story.

———⚬⚬⚬———

I want to thank Jeff Dillow, with KAHN MEDIA, for telling me about the website, Wikimedia Commons. That is where I obtained the picture of the front page of the New York Times that is inserted in this novel. The following is the information from the licensing block that is on the same page as the picture of the newspaper on the website.

This work is in the **public domain** in the United States because it was published (or registered with the U.S. Copyright Office) before January 1, 1928.

———⚬⚬⚬———

BIOGRAPHICAL INFORMATION

Well, Folks, this is novel twelve going to press. YeeeHaw! I will tell you. The original manuscript was completed many years ago. I'm so glad that Julian got to read it before he passed away since I was using his picture as the character of Jonathan in the story. That leaves one more novel that is done but it needs some work. I'm contemplating publishing my short stories as a collection after novel number thirteen is in print. We shall see.

I love it here in Mexico. Moving here after retirement was one of the best decisions I have ever made. To save on my electric bill, I installed forty-one solar panels. It was a no-brainer due to the amount of sun we get here on the SW coast. I calculate that it will take around five and a half years to pay for themselves. The total cost in US dollars was $23,500 and that included installation. Much cheaper than what they would have cost in the States.

I want to mention that the Infinity Publishing Company has gone out of business, so my first two novels published with them are no longer available. I am contemplating republishing them with iUniverse, my current publishing company. We shall see.

PROLOGUE

I have never believed in coincidence. I believe things happen for a reason and we meet the people we do in life for a reason. Also, we meet them when we are supposed to meet them and not before. I believe we're connected to happenings and people in ways that can't necessarily be explained. Certain events, whether large or small, bring certain individuals together. Some may have a big influence on our lives and some not so much but all happen for reasons. Here are some perfect examples.

———— ∞∞ ————

I believe it was in the late 1960s, in Richmond, Virginia, when I went to the Virginia Museum of Fine Arts to see the Salvador Dali jewel collection. I wasn't the only person there to view it.

It was in 1981 in Atlanta, Georgia, when I met Tris. He was the bartender at a wedding reception I was catering at the time. The bride knew him and had asked him to be the bartender.

About a month after meeting, we went to dinner and got into a long conversation. Discussing our histories, we discovered we'd both been in Richmond, during the same time period back in the 1960s. Further discussion somehow brought up the subject of the Dali collection at the museum. We concluded we both had been there and possibly rubbed elbows. But we weren't supposed to meet yet. It wasn't time.

Over the years, Tris and I shared a terrific and very close friendship until I'd never see his handsome, smiling face or hear his unforgettable, deep barrel laugh again. It was August 1ˢᵗ of 1999, just before his birthday on the 4ᵗʰ. He left this life.

———∞∞∞———

In 1977, a friend wanted me to go with him to the Armory, a bar in Atlanta. I didn't want to go, protesting constantly, knowing the night would be a total waste of time. But after much prodding, I finally gave in and went with him.

As my eyes became accustomed to the dim lighting, I looked across the crowded room and saw a man sitting at the bar. He had the similar facial features of the movie actor, Tyrone Power. I could not stop staring at him. Then, most unbelievably, my friend said he happened to know him and introduced me. Had I not gone out that night, I could have missed meeting Phillip, a handsome fireman, the one person who became incredibly significant in my life for nineteen years.

In May of 1996, he caught a cold the stubborn man wouldn't take care of, telling me it would go away. It developed into rampant pneumonia and Phillip went away. He left this life less than a week later on May 10ᵗʰ.

———∞∞∞———

Two years later in 1998, I was working at a transitional home for psychiatric outpatients. The girls who ran the place saw how 'down' I was over losing Phillip. They had the office computer online, so they suggested I do some online dating. I was very reluctant to do so as I thought it outrageous. Now, remember, online dating in 1998 was in its beginnings and not what it is today. Virtually all of the profiles had no pictures, just written descriptions. The girls were adamant and kept pushing. So, I took a leap of faith. I found a personal ad and he sounded nice. So, I responded.

That is how I met Dan. We shared an incredible Platonic relationship for sixteen years. He was a funny, kind, considerate and loving man. We were going to retire together to the SW coast of Mexico. Dan and I loved the ocean and the beach. The area inspired my novels, It Happened In Zihuatanejo, The Quake, Island of the Portal and The Stranger from the Sea. (Presently, they are all in print except for Island of the Portal. It is next after this one.)

It was early May of 2014. We got word our house in Mexico was almost finished. We were so happy and would head down in about six months.

On May 20th, I had fixed breakfast and went to Dan's bedroom to see if he was hungry. I found him in his bed. A heart attack had taken him during the night and he was gone. I'd have to go to our retirement house alone.

Julian's handsome face is similar to that of the character, Jonathan Wolfe, in this novel. I asked him if I could include his picture, so the reader could get an image as to how the character would appear. Thank you, Julian, for letting me use your wonderful picture.

I met Julian online in 2009 after seeing his picture in an online singles ad. He looked much like the character of Daniel in my first published novel, The Old Lighthouse, published in 2007. I wrote to him and sent a quote from the story, describing Daniel. Strangely enough, he wrote back, beginning our friendship. Dan was all for

Julian and me starting a relationship since Dan and I had a Platonic one. After Dan passed away, Julian and I became much closer. I could not believe I had found another incredibly wonderful man with whom I could spend the rest of my life.

But it wasn't meant to be. Julian went in for a simple operation in mid-December of 2017. The operation was a success but he went into an anesthesia coma. He was taken off life support and died on Christmas Day. The world lost an incredible artist that day. I am still trying to deal with his loss.

My novel, <u>Two Portraits in Oil</u>, was published in April of 2020 and is dedicated to him. His picture was used in the design of the front cover. Since that novel was completed in early 2017, Julian got to read it and loved it. He even started calling me Boo, the name the Julian character gives the 'me' character in the book. You have no idea how happy that made me. His face was also used in the front cover design of my novels, <u>The Stranger from the Sea</u>, <u>The Legend of Cavenaugh Island</u> and <u>Saying Goodbye</u>.

My parents were wonderful and amazing people. Interestingly enough, both lived to be ninety-six years old. Dad passed away in 2020. Strangely, Mom passed on March 17th, 2022, which happens to be Dad's Birthday. Yeah. It's like she was planning on surprising him by showing up at his party in the great beyond.

Mrs. Brakebill was a fantastic teacher. I will forever be grateful and in her debt for her support and confidence in me as a writer. I doubt I would have ever considered publishing my writings if not for her encouragement. The world lost an amazing lady when she passed away in November 2021. She is truly missed.

——⌘——

I met Galen Berry online the same way I did Julian. I saw his picture and profile and saw he was a pianist. After some correspondence with one another, I also found out he was extremely good with proofreading and editing. By the way, Galen is still very much alive.

He has been incredibly helpful with my last eight novels. In <u>Saying</u> <u>Goodbye</u>, he suggested an alternative ending to the one I had written. I liked it so much that I completely rewrote the ending to incorporate his suggestion.

I consider myself very lucky to have met him as well as being able to call him my friend. I have also used his picture to represent certain characters in several of my novels. I really appreciate that. Thank you, Galen.

——⌘——

Tris

Phillip

Dan

Julian

My Parents - Marilyn and Gene

My Parents with me and my siblings at Mom and
Dad's 75th Anniversary celebration in 2018
From left to right is me, my brother, Henry who is three
years younger than me, my sister Catherine who is four
years younger than me and my brother, Robert who is five
years younger than me. We siblings are still alive. GRIN

Mrs. Brakebill

Galen

So, you see, those we meet might possibly be the ones who lead us to others who become important. Which fork in the road we choose will determine the direction of our lives. Sometimes, I believe the Fates step in and help us see the right path. It may not be the one we'd planned but later, when we look back, we may actually realize it was the right choice. It's like Dan used to say, quoting the French proverb by Jean de La Fontaine, 'A person often meets his Destiny on the road he took to avoid it.' If we all seriously went about fulfilling our Destiny, there would be no need for the Fates to step in.

Some have asked me if I'd do it all again, knowing the heartache, pain and agony of loss I still endure in seeing those close to me leave me behind. I tell them there's a wonderful country song sung by Garth Brooks whose words go, 'For a moment, all the world was right. How could I have known, that you'd ever say goodbye? And now, I'm glad I didn't know the way it all would end, the way it all would go. Our lives are better left to chance. I could have missed the pain, but I'da had to miss the dance.' They are gone but they still live in my heart and in my mind. Yes, I got to dance with three amazing individuals and I am happy for it. They are immortal as long as they live in my heart, the one who loved them.

And so, this story brings elements of the Fates, timing and the meeting of others, putting them all into play. The places, the people, the circumstances, the events, and maybe even certain numbers, connect them all together to create a certain outcome. An alteration in any of them most likely would significantly change that outcome. Of course, the Fates can step in to hopefully keep things on the right track.

CHAPTER I

Paul opened the door to the main office. Leading Michael in, he pointed to the wall behind the desk. "This, Mister Michael, is what I wanted to show you."

Michael looked at the matted and framed front page of an old newspaper. The paper was yellowed with age but the bold, black headline caused him to start. It was as if a thousand daggers pierced his eyes, his body, his heart. He panted, trying to catch his breath.

"Mister Michael! Are you all right!?" Paul grabbed Michael's arm to steady him.

"I must go! Somehow, I have to try and stop him!" Michael spoke with conviction, turned and ran out of the office.

Paul called out to him, "But where are you going!?"

He yelled loudly, "If I can, I'm saving yesterday!" He ran through the lobby and out the front door.

Paul was unable to run and follow him but knew he was heading to the pavilion. He stopped quickly at the front desk to grab his coat and tell Martin where he was going.

He limped along as fast as he could but grew tired. Halfway there, he needed to pause and rest. Standing at the top of a short flight of stairs in the path, he leaned against the stone balustrade. In his pause, it began to all unfold in his mind, right from the very first day, just almost two weeks earlier when Michael walked into Sandora.

CHAPTER II

It was the spring of 1982 and Michael had been planning this trip for some time now. This was the year of his thirty-sixth birthday. The reason it took so long to come to fruition is because the price of staying at this hotel was not cheap. He wanted to come here due to the wonderful gardens and landscapes that he wanted to paint.

Michael walked through the front doors of the hotel. He stopped for a few moments to look around and absorb the elegance of the large lobby. "Wow!" All he'd heard about the place didn't do it justice. He smiled and headed to the front desk. The sound of his boots on the polished, wooden, parquet floors echoed through the enormous space.

The older gentleman behind the front desk was aware of Michael the moment he entered the building. "Good afternoon, sir. And welcome to Sandora." A warm smile filled his face, "I hope you had a pleasant trip. My name is Paul. And from the things you're carrying, I see you're an artist."

Michael set his large carryall down on the floor and leaned his artist's easel against the front desk. "And a good afternoon to you, too. Yes, I'm an artist. Although there might be those who would differ." He chuckled, "I had a great drive up. I've been so looking forward to this visit. Been saving up for some time to come here. In the brochures for North Carolina, this place looked like some lost and hidden fairytale chateau way up here in the mountains. Looks like it lives up to the concept."

"I think you'll have a wonderful time here. It's quiet and out of the way. There's not that much excitement here for a young man like you. But I think you're here for something more than excitement." Paul looked at the easel. "Since you're here to paint, you'll have many areas that would make great landscape paintings." Paul gave a big smile and stroked his large, bushy, gray-white mustache.

"Yes, I stopped for gas down in town and chatted with the guy at the station. When he realized I was an artist, he said I could probably paint forever here with all the beautiful gardens and scenery. I think he's right."

"If you're really good, the hotel might consider purchasing one to hang." Paul gave a big grin.

"I'm not a professional but I sell one every once in a while. I'm not too bad." He paused for a moment, "Must admit. The architecture here would make a great subject. The light gray, stone walls and the French Gothic windows give it a cathedral quality. The turrets and steep, dark blue-gray slate roofs give it an old-world look. I love the light tan ornamentation. The whole structure seems kidnapped from a fairy story." He looked around the lobby decorated elegantly with gilded French panels accented with oil paintings in wide, gold ornamented frames. A huge, French crystal chandelier, glistening like a thousand sparkling diamonds, hung from the twenty-foot high, ornate ceiling above his head. "Looks like someone stole a wing of Versailles and planted it here."

"Wait till you see all the gardens." Paul added, "A lot of the spring shrubs and bulbs are in bloom. Now, do you have more baggage? I'll get it for you. Sorry, there are no valets. It's the middle of the week and the off-season. Most of the young men are still in school. Usually have them only on weekends or for some major function… till the season picks up again."

"Oh! No problem. I have just a few things still in the car."

"Let me fetch them for you and take them up to your room. Please, sign in if you would."

As Paul walked from behind the desk, he was pushing a small cart to hold Michael's things. That's when Michael noticed he walked with a limp. "Paul, please. I'll get them." He looked down at Paul's leg.

Paul stopped, looked down and patted his left leg, then looked at Michael, "Why, thank you, sir. It's an old injury. Happened right out there in the parking lot. A long time ago." Paul's face flinched suddenly as if recalling some faded memory. He looked hard at Michael. "Excuse me but…" He kept staring at Michael. "Have you ever been here before? Somehow, you look familiar. Like I have met you before."

Michael shook his head and snickered, "Oh, no. No. I've never been here before and I don't think we've ever met. Not to be disrespectful but I could never afford to come here in the past. Took me a while to save up this time." Michael grabbed the cart and headed to his car. "I'll be back in a few minutes and sign in."

Shortly, Michael returned with his artist's case, containing his paints and brushes, a few canvases and a small carryall bag with his turpentine, linseed oil and cleaning rags. On top of the carryall bag was his black cowboy hat. His black boots were placed next to the canvases. The things he'd first brought in he put on the cart. He removed his brown cowboy hat, placing it on the desk then picked up the pen to write his name in the large, hardbound, register book. Three-quarters of it had been filled. He could only imagine the names, the people, filling the previous pages. He resisted the temptation to look back through them. He pulled out his wallet, got out his credit card and placed it on the desk.

Paul kept staring at Michael, at his hat on the desk and back at Michael, "I'm sorry, sir, and I don't mean to be a pest but are you sure we have never met before?" He again looked intensely at Michael's hat on the desk. "I could have sworn." He shook his head as if not being able to recall some distant event.

"I'm pretty sure. Yep. As I said, this place is a bit pricey." Michael nodded politely. "Michael Groves. Please, call me Michael."

Paul looked down at the registry book and the credit card. "Mister Michael Groves. Just a second. Let me check the reservations on the computer. We just got this one in January. They seem to be the new thing. I'm still not real sure how it works. And we still haven't transferred all the information and reservations into it yet. Heard they are the wave of the future and everyone will have one. I think they're a bit pricey, though."

"I believe you're right. I can't afford to buy one. Pretty sure the price will go down as they become more popular. At least, I hope so." Michael agreed.

Paul turned and went to another desk against the wall. He moved the mouse and clicked a few times to finally bring up the reservation page on the monitor. He looked at the screen. "There's a note here. You talked with Martin a few weeks ago. He must have thought you were calling back to confirm. Just a second. There's an asterisk."

"An asterisk? Geez. I hope there isn't a problem."

"Not to worry. We're putting them in if there's some special information we need to check. It means there's a special instruction file in the office, regarding your reservation. I'm sure there isn't a problem. Back in a minute." He went into the main office. After a few minutes, he returned, carrying a file. "Let's see. Michael Groves. Wednesday, April seventh for two weeks. And your reservations have been covered. Paid in advance. Everything. Including all your meals in the dining room. It's all right here."

Michael was shocked and puzzled. "What!? That can't be! Are you sure? But I never paid anything for this visit. Are you sure? Who paid it? I don't understand. Even my meals? There must be some mistake."

"There's a note here in the file approved by top management, indicating that regardless of your expenses, they will all be covered. Carte blanche. They've also put you in one of the finest suites. I have to admit, the card and note are quite old." He turned the old reservation card and note toward Michael.

"Are you absolutely sure? Paul, this is a very expensive hotel. I cannot imagine anyone paying two weeks here for me. Especially, when I have no idea who it is."

"Yes, Mister Michael. Your entire stay. Starting on Wednesday, April seventh, nineteen eighty-two. Today. There's no mistake."

"This never happens to me! How lucky can I be?" Michael shook his head. "Wow! This is really weird. How could anyone have known?" He looked at Paul. "If it does turn out to be an error, I'd still like you to run a charge slip on my card, so the room and any food I eat will be paid for. I don't want anyone to think I'm a mooch."

Paul chuckled, "Mister Michael, I doubt there will be any problem but if you insist, I will."

"Yes, I'd feel a lot better if you did."

Paul ran a charge slip and handed Michael his card back.

"It really is strange. Do you know when it was made?" Michael questioned.

"There's no date or signature on any of the papers. But I assure you, they are authentic and legitimate. They would never be in these files if they weren't."

"This is so crazy. I wasn't even sure I was coming till six months ago. And I wasn't sure of the dates until this past February." He shook his head. "Maybe someone in upper management has a crystal ball."

"You never know, Mister Michael. You never know."

They both could not help but laugh.

Soon, they were standing at the elevators located behind the large grand staircase that came down from the second story.

"You'll be staying in four-o-seven. As I mentioned, it's rather special as it's one of the few on the top floor. The view from the turret windows is quite breathtaking."

Stepping off the elevator, Paul led Michael down a long hall decorated with several alcoves, each containing a beautiful marble statue. "Mister Michael, here's your room. I hope you like it."

When Paul unlocked and opened the door, Michael was amazed. The room was much like a living room with a beautifully carved, marble fireplace mantel. On the other side was a turret space with five narrow, almost floor-to-ceiling windows. The suite was a bedroom, living room and bath. The living room and bedroom were decorated in the French periods of Louis XV and Louis XVI. Gilded panels and moldings were set off by beautiful pastel shades of blue, peach and yellow. French crystal chandeliers hung from the heavily ornamented, high ceilings. Aubusson rugs decorated the parquet floors. Michael grinned, "Wow. I feel like Louis the Fifteenth."

They walked into the bedroom, took everything off the cart and placed them next to the closet doors. Paul turned to Michael. "Will there be anything else?"

"No, thank you, Paul. I appreciate your help." He pulled a five-dollar bill from his wallet and handed it to Paul. "And if you find out who paid for my stay here, let me know and tell them I want to thank them for their incredible generosity."

"Thank you, sir. I will. And if you should need anything, please don't hesitate to ring down. And here is your key." Paul handed Michael the key, took hold of the cart and left the room, closing the door behind him.

The drive up from Atlanta had been exhausting. Since it was just mid-afternoon, there definitely was time to take a short rest. He closed the drapes over the windows in the bedroom to block out the afternoon light and turned on the chandelier in the room. A nice hot shower made him realize how tired he really was. A short nap before dinner would be just what he needed. After dinner, he would come back and get a good night's sleep to be well-rested for the next day's adventures. He closed the bedroom door, walked over to the bed, plumped a pillow and got in. Almost before he knew it, he was asleep.

CHAPTER III

When Michael opened his eyes, the chandelier was still on. He'd forgotten to turn it off before lying down. He looked over at the large clock on the dresser. "Humm. Almost six-thirty. That's cool." He mumbled, "I'll just run downtown to a take-out service and grab a quick bite before I head to bed." He knew the dining room was probably an elegant place and didn't want to dress up right then. He would save that for the weekend.

He began to plan his itinerary in his head for the following day. He definitely wanted to get an early start in the morning, so he could see the area and find a few places that would make nice paintings.

He opened his carry bag and pulled out some clean jeans and shirt. Finally, he was dressed and ready to head out the door. Before he opened it, he could see himself in the large mirror, hanging on the door. He was wearing his fleece-lined jeans jacket, red flannel shirt, jeans, boots and his brown cowboy hat. It was his persona. He had never been to a Wild West ranch but this style of attire was something he liked and felt comfortable in. He smiled, stroked his dark brown mustache and beard then opened the door.

Coming out of the elevator, he rounded the grand staircase and headed to the front desk. He saw Paul standing behind it. "Paul! Do you ever go home?" He chuckled.

Paul looked up and grinned, "Ah! Mister Michael. And where are you headed so early this morning?"

Michael stopped in his tracks. "Morning?" Michael was totally surprised, "What do you mean, morning?"

Paul looked at him strangely, "Why, it's a little after seven. Yes. In the morning."

Michael tilted his head back. "Damn! I had no idea I was THAT tired." He started shaking his head as he looked at Paul. "I took a nap and was going to get up and run downtown for a quick bite before heading to bed but it seems I slept through the whole thing." He started snickering, "Geez."

"Would you like to have a cup of coffee and a sweet roll with me? Go sit over there near the fireplace. I'll bring everything there in a minute."

"That would be terrific. Thanks, Paul. But what about the front desk?"

"Not to worry. Martin is in the office and will take care of things. It's so early, doubtful anyone will be coming to the desk."

Shortly, Paul walked up and placed a tray on the coffee table in front of Michael. He sat down across from him and fixed them both a cup. "Have a nice roll. They're very good."

Soon, they started chatting.

Before Michael realized, he was telling Paul his life story. Paul didn't mind. He was a good listener and even though he'd only known Michael for less than a day, he sensed there was something different about him. He could feel his sincerity, openness and amiable personality.

Michael found it easy to talk to Paul. It was like talking with his long-lost grandfather. He found himself telling Paul things he thought he would never tell just anyone. And it was comfortable, "Sorry. I guess I got into motormouth mode. Was curious. Don't mean to pry but how did you hurt your leg?"

"It was a long time ago." Paul looked up into space, seeming to search for something in his head, "Back in nineteen twenty. August twenty-fourth, actually. I was eleven, going on twelve. Was out in the parking lot. One of the guests hit me with his car. It was my fault. I ran out in front of it, chasing after a ball I was playing with. Unfortunately, it never healed quite right. Had the limp ever since."

"Damn. Sorry about that."

"So, what's on your agenda today? Wait till you see the gardens. We also have horseback riding. There are trails up into the hills and around the lake. I think you'll find many places you might like to set your easel up and paint."

"Well, I guess I should get started. Thank you so much again for the coffee and rolls. See you later on."

———⟨∞⟩———

All day Thursday, Michael chose a few places he wanted to paint. One, in particular, was a large pavilion, that seemed to hide in the far reaches of the garden, overlooking the lake. It was down from the hotel and of the same ornate architecture. To Michael, there was a comparison. His vacation to France a few years earlier came to mind. The pavilion was to the hotel as the Petit Trianon is to the Palace of Versailles.

It was Friday morning and down the paths he walked, carrying his easel, canvas and paintbox until he came to a spot where he could see the pavilion in the distance. It was across an inlet and at such an angle that captured most of its architectural beauty, nestled among the surrounding trees and flowering shrubs with the mountains in the distance across the lake. The sun was cooperating beautifully. He finished applying the final colors on his palette. A few quick pencil lines for placement and composition then it was time for brush and paint. He worked all morning, applying paint to the canvas.

He thought of Claude Monet doing several canvases, each capturing a specific period of time and the changing light on the west front of Rouen Cathedral. For Michael, the altering light and shadows on the pavilion and the plantings only gave him a greater selection of colors for his single canvas.

By the late afternoon, his painting was virtually finished. Michael was quite pleased with it and was amazed at how quickly it flowed onto the canvas. It was virtually complete, capturing the beautiful colors of the azaleas and other blooming plants surrounding the elegant structure. He knew it was going to look great in a nice wide, ornate, gold leaf frame.

As he entered the lobby, he was aware of more guests arriving at the hotel for the weekend. He looked over at the reception desk and saw Paul busy with guests checking in.

"I want to see that when you're finished!" Paul called out with a big grin on his face.

"Okay! Will do!" Michael nodded his head and kept heading to the elevators.

Michael had been doing fast food since he arrived, running down into town. He knew he could have eaten in the dining room but didn't want to abuse his privilege. But tonight, Paul indicated the dining room would be open late, with the number of guests arriving for the weekend. And there would be dancing, too. Since he had not seen the dining room yet, all he could imagine were the ones at such places as the Ritz, the Waldorf Astoria and other such elegant places where dining and dancing were the norm. He would dress for the occasion.

The next elevator was empty. He was glad as he didn't want to get paint on any of the guests much less smear his painting.

Arriving in his rooms, he set up his easel in the living room and placed the painting on it. He stood back and looked at it. "Not bad. Not bad at all."

He went to the bedroom, laid out his clothes for dinner and decided to take a quick nap. After a hot shower, he set the small alarm clock he'd brought with him and went to bed. He didn't want a repeat of the previous Wednesday night.

CHAPTER IV

When Michael opened his eyes, he looked at the clock on the dresser and was surprised to see it was almost seven o'clock. He reached over and shut off his alarm clock before it had time to go off.

Since it was the beginning of the weekend and his first night in the hotel dining room, he decided to dress well. He wanted to look like he belonged, knowing full well that this was an expensive hotel and those who would be eating in the dining room that night would be people of means, not someone like him who in reality could only afford peanut butter and jelly sandwiches. He took his time. He didn't want to get there too early. He remembered there was going to be dancing. True, he was not going to dance as he had no partner but he liked to watch, especially if it was a nice ballroom style. He smiled, recalling an early memory when he had taken ballroom dancing when he was very young.

It was almost eight o'clock when he headed for the door. Again, he saw his reflection in the big mirror. It was an average built man, five and a half feet tall, dressed in black formal pants, black jacket, white ruffled shirt, black bow tie and cummerbund and of course, his more formal, black cowboy hat and boots. Michael knew he always looked good in black since it complemented his dark brown hair, mustache and beard.

Walking down the hall, the sound of his boots was cushioned by the thick carpet runners. He took the elevator to the second floor and got off. He'd thought about doing something really crazy ever since he saw the staircase. A devilish sense went through him.

Finally, he was standing some ten feet from the top of the stairs. He could hear the echoes of a piano in some distant place.

Looking down and out across the large lobby, he envisioned a scene from an old television show with Loretta Young, whirling down the stairs in a beautiful gown. He began to laugh, suppressing his feminine side to swirl down the steps, "What would people think? But it is nineteen eighty-two." He continued to chuckle, "But not right now." He descended the steps without fanfare.

There were several, well-dressed people in the lobby, heading toward the dining room. The sound of a piano was coming from that direction.

Michael entered the reception area to the dining room and removed his hat. He waited patiently for his turn to be seated. He couldn't see the whole dining room from where he was but there were the sounds of mixed conversations, laughter and the occasional tinkling of glassware.

Finally, a man came over and bowed slightly. He looked around to see if anyone was with Michael but realized he was alone. "Dinner for one, sir?"

"Yes, thank you." Entering the dining room, he noticed a wall of French doors and windows. "Excuse me. Would it be possible to sit at the windows?"

"Very good, sir." He slowly led Michael through the lavishly decorated room to a small table near the large windows and doors that could open out onto the terrace beyond. The light given off by the gas lamps around the terrace made it possible to see several wrought iron tables and chairs outside. But the cool night air made it too uncomfortable to sit outside for dinner.

Soon, he noticed several guests looking at him. He rather

expected it since he wasn't wearing the conventional evening wear like everyone else.

The spacious room, decorated in the French style, had a fairly large area for dancing. A very talented young man in evening clothes was playing the grand piano near the dance floor. The music was varied and quite enjoyable, nothing outrageous or with a fast tempo.

Paul would explain later that a rather prestigious liberal arts college was located in the area and many of the talented music students would come to the hotel and perform. Mostly, these were students on scholarships who really needed extra money.

He began with his usual Old Fashioned before dinner. He decided to take his time with dinner. No rushing. He would have a few cocktails and listen to the superb piano music. The meal was exceptional. Since he had spent so much time occupying the table, he left a large tip for his waiter before getting up to leave. Then, he went over and dropped several dollar bills into the tip goblet on the piano. The young man nodded and smiled his appreciation. He walked over to the host. He handed the host his signed bill. "Thank you very much. The meal was excellent. And the music was superb."

"I'm glad you enjoyed it, sir. We'll see you tomorrow night?"

"Yes." Michael smiled, "I look forward to it."

Michael returned to his room. Even though he'd taken the short nap earlier, he was still quite tired. A good night's rest is exactly what he needed. Before he turned out the light, he looked at the clock on the dresser. It was a little after eleven-thirty. He had no idea it was that late. He decided to blame it on the number of cocktails he'd consumed. Shortly, he was asleep.

CHAPTER V

The next day, he dressed in his jeans and flannel shirt then put on his jacket. His casual brown boots and hat were the usual. As he left the room, he grabbed another canvas, paint box and easel and headed to the door. As he did, his eyes glanced at the mantle clock in the living room area. It was almost eight forty-five.

He stopped by the front desk to speak to Paul, "Dinner last night was great. I loved the piano music. I have to say, I'm truly super impressed with everything."

Seeing Michael with all his art supplies, Paul grinned, "I saw you had your painting yesterday. Is it finished?"

"Almost." Michael was telling a little white lie. The canvas was complete. He just didn't want anyone to see it without a frame.

"I really want to see it when it's done." Paul was very happy.

"Will do." He nodded his head. "Talk with you later."

"Looks like a beautiful day out there. See you later." Paul waved as Michael headed out the door.

He went to another place he had picked to paint and spent the rest of the day there. During the day, several of the guests, strolling in the gardens, passed by and commented on the beauty of his work. A few even asked if he'd consider a commission and took his personal card. His mind pondered the outcome, "I should consider coming here more often. Who knows where some of these commissions might lead? Oh, yeah."

The afternoon passed and it was time to get back. He packed up everything. Soon, he was passing through the lobby.

"Mister Michael! Good afternoon. How did things go today?"

Michael walked over and did something he rarely did. He turned the nearly finished canvas toward Paul. "A few folks came by and saw my work. I think I might get a few commissions. And this one isn't even finished yet."

"That's terrific. You would be surprised how many come from long distances to stay here. A lot of them are quite wealthy. We even have many guests from Europe. During the summer, you can find people from major cities all over the world here on vacation. Many return again and again. Some families have been coming here for generations. You never know. You could get a lot of commissions for paintings."

"That would be great." Michael gave a 'thumbs-up'. "Think I'll go up and get ready for dinner. Talk with you soon." Michael turned and went to his rooms.

After a long shower, he decided to take another nap before dinner. He set his alarm clock and soon was asleep.

CHAPTER VI

When he awoke, it was after seven. He dressed in his all-black again, donned his hat and headed to the dining room. "I don't care if they think these are the only really uptown clothes I own."

As he walked into the reception area, he removed his hat and noticed the host was not the same one as the previous evening. The music was different, too. Tonight there were several other musicians, accompanying the piano. The number of dinner guests seemed to be larger. "Maybe it's because it's Saturday evening."

"Good evening." He spoke to the host, "One for dinner. I was wondering if it might be possible to sit at a small table next to the windows?"

"Certainly, sir. May I take your hat?" The young man gestured at the hat.

"That's all right. I'll put it on the other chair at my table."

"Very good, sir." He led him to a table as requested.

Michael noticed everyone in the room seemed to be watching him walk to his table. It was a similar feeling as the previous evening but something was different. He realized his attire was a far cry from the very formal dress of the other guests. But the feeling was fleeting. He was who he was and he brushed it off. He placed his hat on the chair opposite from where he was getting ready to sit down. Already on the table in front of him was the menu for the evening.

"We'll be with you very shortly, sir." The young man bowed slightly and left the table.

Within a few moments, a waiter arrived. "May I get you something to drink, sir?"

"Oh. Yes, thank you. That would be great. I'd like to have an Old Fashioned, please."

The waiter smiled, bowed slightly and left the table.

Michael began to slowly relax and take in his surroundings. He had deliberately picked a chair from where he could get the best view of the whole room and its occupants. It was interesting. On closer look, everyone's attire was very tailored but seemed somewhat dated for both the men and the women. He whispered, "Damn, have I crashed a Roaring Twenties theme party?" Most looked at him a little strangely with his black cowboy hat and boots. But they smiled and just accepted his difference.

Within a few minutes, the waiter brought Michael's drink. "I'll return shortly to get your order."

"Please, take your time. I'm in no hurry this evening." Michael smiled up at the waiter.

"Very good, sir." He smiled, bowed slightly and walked away.

Michael took a sip then spoke quietly, "Damn, what a great Old Fashioned. Think it's the best one I've ever had. Better than the one last night. Must be another bartender." He held the glass off and looked at it. "Yeah. Great Old Fashioned."

He turned and happened to glance out the window. Down, out and across the inlet of the lake, he could see light in the windows of the pavilion. He spoke softly with a giggle, "Hey. Somebody's home." His face was filled with a huge grin, "It sure didn't look that way when I was checking it out the other day before I did the painting. They were probably at work."

After a moment, he picked up the menu to see the available

selections for the evening. "The chicken sounds really good." He mumbled, "Humm. Just like an expensive hotel and dining room. No prices on the menu." His mind questioned, "But that's strange. There were prices on the one last night. Maybe they don't put them on the menu for the weekend. Don't want to shock the patrons." He began to giggle again, "Oh, well. I think I am glad my meals are covered." After a further look at the selections, he made his decision. He set the menu down on the corner of the table and leaned back in his chair, so he could take in more of his surroundings.

He began to look around the room, noticing several couples on the dance floor under the large chandelier. The soft light in the room and the slow tempo of the music made the room feel warm and cozy.

Suddenly, Michael saw a man in evening clothes with dark, virtually black hair, parted on the right side, sitting alone almost diagonally across the room. The man was looking right at him. Michael usually liked those with dark eyes but this combination of dark hair and intense green eyes was mesmerizing. The man's left eye was covered with a black patch. His dark mustache and neatly trimmed beard slightly shadowed the man's smile. He kept smiling at Michael until he realized Michael was finally aware of his stare.

Michael smiled back and bowed his head slightly. The man bowed his head and his smile turned into a big grin. The man picked up his cocktail, raising it slightly in a subtle toast toward Michael. Michael returned the gesture with his Old Fashioned.

Michael thought how good-looking the man was, "Wonder what happened to his eye?" He looked down at the table, shaking his head slightly. "But does he have any personality… or a brain?" He slowly shook his head. "Yeah. So many good-looking men are such total self-centered airheads." At that moment, the waiter walked up. He looked up at the waiter. "Could I have another, please? And tell the bartender this has to be one of the best Old Fashioneds I've ever had."

"Yes. Of course, sir. Thank you. I'm sure he'll be pleased with the compliment." The waiter bowed and walked away.

Michael kept perusing the room but couldn't help returning to look at the man across the room. He noticed the man gesture to Michael's waiter to come to his table, say something to him, hand him something then let him go.

Not long afterward, Michael's waiter returned with his Old Fashioned. He left but returned shortly with a bottle of wine in a chilling bucket. The young man opened it. "Sir, the bartender wanted to thank you very much for your kind comment. And the wine was sent to you for dinner. The gentleman wanted me to tell you he's ordering dinner for you tonight and is taking care of everything. He hopes you'll enjoy it."

"The gentleman? The bartender?"

"Oh. No, sir. The gentleman. Yes, sir. Mister Jonathan."

"Mister Jonathan?"

"Yes, sir. Mister Jonathan is the man sitting over there across the room." He turned in the direction of the man sitting alone. "He instructed me to tell you."

Michael looked over and saw the man smiling, slightly raising his glass. "Interesting. So, HE's Mister Jonathan." Michael responded in kind with his drink.

All through dinner, Michael couldn't help himself and kept looking over to see the handsome man across the room still periodically glancing at him. "If he's an airhead, he's not one when it comes to choosing a wine. And his choice of foods was beyond belief. Damn. It was excellent." He had to chuckle to himself when suddenly, the words to a song from 'South Pacific' came to his mind. He whispered the words with melody, "'Some enchanted evening... you will see a stranger... You will see a stranger... across a crowded room.'" He had to make a concerted effort not to start laughing.

The waiter was extremely attentive, filling his wine glass the moment it was nearing empty. Michael never had to touch the bottle.

After the waiter removed the dishes from the table, he returned with another Old Fashioned and a small sealed envelope, placing both on Michael's table. "This is from Mister Jonathan, sir. He told me to tell you not to worry about a tip before you leave. He will take care of it. I will tell you, too, that Mister Jonathan is very generous with his gratuities."

"Thank you. Please, tell Mister Jonathan, I truly appreciate his generosity and his excellent selection of wine and food."

The waiter walked in the direction of the handsome man across the room. Michael discreetly raised his cocktail in a toast. He watched the waiter say something to the gentleman and leave the table. The man smiled and similarly raised his cocktail.

Michael picked up the small envelope and opened it. It was a short note.

'I hope your meal was satisfactory. Max is a superb chef and is absolutely marvelous with food. You look like you could be an interesting man. I did not order you dessert. I wondered if you might like to join me for that, have a drink and talk. I live on the north side of the lake in the cottage behind the stone wall. If you look out the windows, you can see the lights on there. If so, come by around eleven.... Jonathan Wolfe'

"Oh." He mumbled, "Jonathan is his first name. Okay." Michael turned, looked at Jonathan and nodded his head in the affirmative. Jonathan bowed slightly. Michael looked back at the note again. He chuckled to himself, "Cottage. Yeah. Sure. Believe it. It's the pavilion I painted the other day." He looked out the window in the direction of the pavilion. "If that's his definition of a cottage, I live in a damn shack." Again, he had to contain himself from laughing.

Michael realized the note indicated discretion. He folded it and put it in his jacket pocket. Standing to leave the dining room, he turned toward Jonathan's table and slightly bowed his head. Passing through the entrance, he thanked the host and indicated the excellence of the food, service and music.

As he approached the grand staircase, he started up slowly, forgetting about the elevators. He couldn't get Jonathan out of his mind. He wondered what his voice sounded like and how tall he was. Entering his rooms, he got out of his dress clothes and put on a deep red, plaid, flannel shirt, his jeans and brown boots. Next, he put on his fleece jacket and brown cowboy hat. Standing in front of the mirror, he was rather pleased with what he saw. A quick turn to check the time showed he had twenty minutes to get to the pavilion. He would take his time.

He went down, out the side door and onto the terrace. The exterior gaslights were dim but Michael could see his way across the terrace, down the stairs to the pathways and stairways below. Ornamental gas lamps illuminated the path along the way. He remembered the way to the pavilion from the day he painted it.

Arriving, he unlatched the iron gate in the stone wall around the yard. The sound of his boots resounded on the flagstone walkway.

He walked up to the large wooden door, grabbed the large brass knocker and pounded three times.

Shortly, the door opened and there stood Jonathan, over six feet tall, still in his evening wear. A big smile filled his face. He extended his hand as he greeted Michael in a calm deep voice, "Well. Hello, cowboy. I'm Jonathan Wolfe. Please, come in. I'm so glad you came." The sound and tone of his voice reminded Michael of Sam Elliott's in the 1976 movie, 'Lifeguard'.

Michael smiled, shaking Jonathan's hand, "Michael. Michael Groves. And thank you so much for dinner. Very generous and gracious of you. It was incredible."

"Max is a true treasure when it comes to preparing food. Wait until you taste the dessert he prepared for us." He led the way to the large living room. "Please, have a seat. Your drink is on the table. Old Fashioned isn't it?"

"Yes. Thank you." Michael expressed his appreciation, sat down and started looking around the room.

"Please, excuse me while I go and change. I'll be down in a few minutes and we'll have that dessert." Jonathan headed for the spiral staircase, located in the large turret tower in the corner of the living room.

Michael noticed the room was filled with antiques many in the French styles. Many beautiful Aubusson rugs were on the floors. Crystal chandeliers and light fixtures gave the room a soft glow.

Within a few minutes, Jonathan returned wearing some casual safari-type clothing. "I'm glad you accepted my offer to visit. Wasn't sure you'd really follow through." He went to a small bar cabinet, fixed a drink for himself and dished the dessert onto plates. He walked over to Michael and handed him a plate. There was an incredible chocolate fantasy on it. "If you like chocolate, you're going to be amazed at this dessert. Max calls it his 'Chocolate Surprise'. It is something amazingly delectable."

Michael took his fork and placed some of the dessert in his mouth. "Oh… my… God! This is…" He paused slightly, "There are no words." He ate some more.

"I told you." Jonathan began to chuckle.

Finishing, Jonathan took the plates and put them on the bar. He returned to his seat across from Michael. "I'm so glad you came."

"I truly appreciate the invite. When I was down in this area a few days ago, I didn't realize it was a residence or occupied. You have a beautiful house. I wanted to paint it. On canvas, of course."

"So, you're an artist? I'd like to see your work sometime." He looked at Michael's glass. "How's your drink? Is it to your liking?"

"It's terrific." Michael kept looking around the room. He was quite impressed with the richness of the ornamentation and furnishings. The entire interior was elegant, yet it still had a masculine feel.

To Michael, Jonathan appeared to be just a little older than himself and seemed to have an open, laid-back demeanor.

Jonathan spoke, "I see you looking around. Would you like to see the cottage?"

"That would be terrific. Would you mind? I'd love to."

Jonathan was upfront and free with the showing, describing many of the focal points throughout the first story: the dining room, library, billiard room and office. Completing the walk, he led Michael back to the living room. "Please, have a seat while I stoke the fire." He headed toward the fireplace. "Another drink?"

"Yes, thank you." One thing Michael noticed on the tour was

the lack of a kitchen. But he realized the proximity of the pavilion to the hotel and the dining room there. And of course, Jonathan would have food brought down. There was no need for a kitchen.

Then, Michael asked about the pavilion, "I noticed the pavilion... the cottage... is of the same architecture and materials as the hotel. Was it built at the same time?"

"Oh, no. I had it built almost eight years ago. Since it was so close to the hotel and I like the style of the hotel, it was only fitting they blend. I obtained many of the materials from the same places the hotel did. Like the stone. It's from the same quarry the stone for the hotel was cut." He handed Michael an Old Fashioned then sat on the settee across from Michael, sitting in a French fauteuil. "So, when will you start the painting? Of the cottage?"

Michael bent his head down. Yeah. He did indicate he wanted to paint it but how could Jonathan know he definitely would? But anyone could see the cottage... the pavilion... would make a great painting. It's why he chose it to do first. He looked right at Jonathan. "Well, to be honest, it's done. I have it in my room."

"Really!?" Jonathan yelled out in total surprise, "I'd like to see it."

"Well, I guess I'll have to show it to you some time."

Jonathan chuckled, "I dabble a little but my work is not very good. No insecurities here. Just knowledge of the truth. But I will say in attempting, I have a greater appreciation for a good painting, the work and talent it took to complete it."

Michael responded, "I know what you mean. I play 'at' the piano. Makes me appreciate anyone who is truly accomplished at the keyboard. Do you play?" His eyes turned to the large grand embraced in the curve of the staircase. He shook his head. "Guess that was a stupid question with that grand over there."

Jonathan nodded. "Yes, I do."

"Why don't you play something? Would love to hear you." Michael was somewhat insistent.

Jonathan went and sat at the piano. He turned and smiled at Michael, "Now, remember. You did ask."

Several shorter pieces of Chopin, Liszt and Debussy filled the room.

Michael was quite impressed with Jonathan's talent. "You play exceedingly well. Do you concertize?" Michael applauded.

"Oh, no. I'm not that good."

"That's what you say. As far as I'm concerned, you can play the piano anytime you want for me. Anytime."

Their light conversation continued. Then, Jonathan looked over at the French clock on the mantle. "I can't believe it. It's almost two-thirty in the morning. Didn't mean to keep you up so late."

"Not a problem. Hey! I'm on vacation. Not on any schedule." Michael responded, "I'll be here till Thursday, the twenty-second and I'm going to enjoy every minute of it."

"Michael, if you don't want to go back to the hotel, you can stay the night here if you like. You can sleep in the second bedroom. And something to think about. I'm going horseback riding tomorrow and would like you to join me. You seem to be dressed for it already." Jonathan referred to the clothes Michael was wearing.

"Hey!" Michael clapped his hands. "I'd like that. It's been some time since I've ridden. Sounds like fun."

"So, I guess we shall call it an evening and continue tomorrow. Let's head upstairs."

They went upstairs and Jonathan showed Michael the room

where he was to sleep. They walked through a door to the bathroom. "I hope you don't mind but it's the same one I use from my room."

"I don't mind at all."

"And there's some soap, towels and the like in the closet." He went into the closet and brought out a new toothbrush, handing it to Michael. Then, he pointed out several things in the room. "Feel free to use what you need. The tooth powder is in that container." He pointed to a ceramic container near the sink. "See you in the morning." Jonathan headed for another door. "Goodnight. I'm really glad you came."

"Goodnight. I appreciate the invitation and I'm glad I'm here, too. And thank you again for dinner. That was very considerate of you."

"You're more than welcome. My pleasure." He opened the door, went through it and closed it.

Michael prepared for bed after Jonathan left. He used the toothbrush Jonathan had given him. The tooth powder in the ceramic container turned out to be quite gritty. "Guess I'll have to bring mine if I get to visit again."

Getting in bed, the cool sheets felt good against his naked body. He hated wearing pajamas or underwear to bed. It was something that started back during his college days, so he slept naked. He had Jan, his roommate at that time, to thank for it.

Lying there in the dark, he thought out loud, "What a terrific guy. I believe we could become friends, good friends. But, damn! He seems to have a lot of money. A lot more than I do. But he doesn't seem to be snobby about it. I don't think he'd have invited me here if he were. What can I say? Oh, well. We shall see." He stared into the darkness. "I'm just going to enjoy the time." He was quiet and finally asleep.

CHAPTER VII

When Michael opened his eyes, the house was quiet. Light, coming through the beveled glass windows, sent sprays of rainbow color throughout the room.

"I wonder if Jonathan's up?" He got out of bed and put on his jeans. "Wonder what time it is?" He went to the bathroom door and knocked.

A voice came from the other side, "Michael, good morning! I'm getting ready to take a shower and shave."

"That's fine. I'll wait till you're done. I just wanted to brush my teeth and shave." Michael talked through the closed door, "By the way, where did you buy that tooth powder? It's gritty as hell."

"Come in. What was that?"

Michael entered the bathroom. "I was making a comment about your tooth powder. If I get to visit again, I'll bring mine. I think you'll like it much better. Trust me. I was going to shave but realized I don't have my razor with me."

"Sounds good. I'll loan you my razor and I'll get the lather ready. You can shave while I take a shower. And what do you shave anyway?" Jonathan stared at Michael's face full of fur.

"Oh. I shave my neck. That's all."

Jonathan was adjusting the water in the shower, standing completely naked except for his eye patch and a large gold medallion on a simple gold chain around his neck. Michael could see Jonathan's body had thick coal-black hair covering the chest, stomach, lower arms and legs of his muscular body. It was significantly more than the hair on his own body.

"Well, I was wondering how tall you really were. I mean, without your boots." Jonathan looked down at Michael. "Seems I'm somewhat bigger than you are." He flexed his eyebrows several times.

Michael looked Jonathan up and down. "From what I can see, you're a lot bigger than me…" He paused for a moment, "Yeah. In more ways than one." He gave a huge Cheshire Cat grin.

Jonathan looked at Michael's grinning face then realized the reference. They both began to snicker that turned into full-blown laughter.

"All right. Let's get back to the task at hand." Jonathan opened the door to the cabinet under the counter and pulled out a mug with a brush and a straight razor. Setting the razor on the counter, he turned on the hot water faucet at the sink. Shortly, he had whipped a rich lather in the mug. "Here you go." He handed the mug to Michael.

Michael was stunned. He'd never used a straight razor before in his life. But trying not to appear stupid, he picked up the razor. "Thank you."

"Hope you're not offended but I take off my patch when I shower."

"Of course not. Pretend I'm not here."

Jonathan looked Michael up and down, standing there in just his jeans. A huge grin covered his face, "Sure. That's easier said than done." He flexed his eyebrows several times. He took off his eye patch, setting it on the cabinet then returned to the shower and closed the curtain. He began humming some tune quickly distorted by the water spray.

Michael used the brush to cover his neck with lather. After a few minutes, he started with the razor. He took a few strokes. It was immediately evident, he would never be able to master a straight razor. A few more strokes and he had to stop. The blade was very sharp and his neck was not lucky. Several drops of blood appeared where he had nicked himself. "Oh, well. Better luck next time. If there is a next time." He said softly.

Jonathan finished with the shower and dried himself as Michael wiped off the remaining lather. "Now, it's my turn." Jonathan whipped up more lather, looked in the mirror and with the speed and accuracy of a great sculptor, moved the razor over the surface of his skin, not touching his mustache or beard.

Michael stood in amazement. Jonathan hadn't drawn the first drop of blood. "Practice makes perfect, I guess." He muttered, "And he does it with only one eye. Damn."

"What?" Jonathan looked at Michael reflected in the mirror above the counter.

"Oh, nothing. Just talking to myself. Think I'll take a quick shower, too, if it's all right."

"Sure. I'll be in my room getting dressed." Jonathan left the room.

Michael took his shower. As he dried off, he pressed small pieces of toilet paper on the cuts on his neck. He stood at the closed door to Jonathan's bedroom. "I'll go finish getting dressed and meet you in the hall." He headed to his room.

"All right. Be there in a minute."

After dressing, he removed the pieces of toilet paper from his neck as the bleeding had stopped.

Within a few minutes, they met in the hall outside the bedrooms.

Jonathan was wearing a pair of riding pants, boots, a long sleeve, buttoned white shirt and a dark, wool, double-breasted jacket. "Let's go get some breakfast and then we'll go riding. There are several places I think you will enjoy seeing. Some might inspire you for a painting."

"Nice riding outfit." Michael mumbled to himself, "Really uptown. And I look like country come to town."

They left the pavilion through the French doors onto the east terrace. From there, they went down the steps to a path that wound through the landscape and through a small gate in the stone wall. This path finally joined the path that went around the inlet of the lake and finally, right up to the steps of the terrace of the hotel dining room.

When they entered the dining room, Jonathan waved to a man across the room, "Good morning, Max. Something quick and easy for my friend and me."

Max was a stocky gentleman, of medium height, clean-shaven except for a large, bushy mustache and dark brown hair parted in the middle. Michael thought he looked to be in his later thirties. One of his most outstanding features was his infectious smile. For some strange reason, an image of Paul popped into his mind. He pondered it for a moment then dismissed it.

"Good morning, Mister Jonathan. Certainly. Right away."

Michael noticed a slight accent in Max's voice. He wasn't sure but thought it could possibly be German.

Jonathan led Michael to the table where he was seated the previous evening. "Have a seat." They both sat down.

Within a few minutes, Max arrived with two cups of coffee, small plates and a basket of hot rolls. Setting them down, he was gone only a short time before returning with sugar, creamer and a container of dark marmalade. "I'll have your ham and eggs, shortly."

"Thank you, Max. Oh, Max, this is my friend, Michael. We're going riding today."

Max looked out the wall of French windows. "It looks like a fine day for riding."

Michael spoke up, "Max, I wanted to compliment you on dinner last night. It was absolutely excellent. And your chocolate dessert was unbelievable. Thank you."

Max gave a big grin, "Thank you, Mister Michael. I appreciate it. They are my own recipes. I'm so glad you liked it." He looked over at Jonathan. "Looks to be a very fine day." Max winked his right eye, smiled, bowed his head slightly and left the table.

Michael looked at Jonathan. "I'm so sorry. I wasn't thinking when I spoke of the dessert. I didn't mean to break a confidence."

"Don't worry. Max knew I was inviting you to the cottage last night for dessert. I sent him a note with your waiter. Right after I saw you when we discreetly toasted one another. I wasn't sure you would come but I had hopes and wanted to be prepared if you did. He knew I wanted something really special. He gave me the chocolate dessert just as I was leaving the dining room last night. Max knows me well and is not judgmental and doesn't jump to any conclusions. His wink was a sign he approves. But thank you for your concern."

Michael wanted to know what that meant but didn't want to ruffle any feathers. He kept silent.

Michael and Jonathan finished breakfast and headed for the stables. The stable master had two horses ready. A sleek black horse was Jonathan's regular ride. A palomino was saddled for Michael.

"Mount up, Michael. We should be back by late afternoon. Wait till you see the places I want to show you. I hope you like them as much as I do." They slowly headed up a mountain path.

After an hour, they came to a beautiful stream and waterfall. Jonathan dismounted and let his horse drink. He sat on a nearby rock. Michael joined him while letting his horse get a drink of water, too.

"I love this place. The sound of the pouring water is so relaxing. I sometimes come here in the summer and stretch out in the water under the fall. Sometimes the craziness of business and travel makes me insane. This place is like a refuge. Actually, all the places I will show you today are special to me."

Michael smiled, "Okay. I guess it's my turn. There was a place we used to go when I was a teenager. It was back in the swamp at home. Several of us would swim during the summer. Do I dare tell you we did it without clothes?"

"We?" Jonathan flashed a huge Cheshire Cat grin, "I know there's more to this story." He clapped his hands together.

Michael flushed, slightly embarrassed, "I'll explain sometime. The mental image and lurid scenario are far better than the actuality." He just grinned.

"What would you say to coming here in the summer and swimming with me?" His eyes grew big and joy filled his face, "Without clothes!"

Michael was rather surprised at how open and forward Jonathan was. It seemed if he wanted to say it, he did. This trait Michael really liked. He'd known many who were so indecisive and could never speak their mind. And it drove him crazy. "Well." Michael paused for a moment, "I think that could be a lot of fun. But you don't even know me. I might be some axe murderer."

"I doubt that." He smiled, "I'm a pretty good judge of character and can usually tell a lot about a person very quickly. I have to. I've had to learn to very quickly sum up a person. It may not seem fair or kind but it is necessary. Especially, in business."

"Okay. If you're so good at that, how do you see me?" Michael threw his shoulders back, crossed his arms and gave a confident grin, thinking Jonathan would never be able to see the person within him.

Jonathan looked very hard at Michael before he began to speak, "What I'm going to say isn't to hurt you or make you uneasy. But I want you to know what I see and what I feel about you, holding nothing back. Will you be comfortable with that?"

"All right, Mister Sherlock Holmes. Go at it." Michael was sure Jonathan could never guess the really personal things about himself.

"Are you sure?" Jonathan asked again.

"Go for it." Michael was sure Jonathan would miss the mark by a mile.

"I'll begin by saying our talk last night was light and never really touched on things about the inner person but I did get some feelings and thoughts. So, let me begin."

For the next several minutes, Jonathan went into his impressions. Michael was taken totally by surprise. He read him like an open book.

Jonathan started off by explaining how he saw Michael's status both economically and socially, realizing he was the perfect example of the starving artist. Then, he began to analyze his private life and brought out the facts of his failed relationships, his great desire to find someone to share his life with and his desire to find and know real love. He pointed out that even though he could project a sense of confidence, deep down he was quite insecure about many things regarding himself. Jonathan completely dissected his whole life right in front of him like peeling away the leaves of a head of lettuce, until he had reached the inner core.

Michael was totally shocked and overwhelmed. It was as if he'd worn his whole life on his sleeve. It was rather unsettling and disconcerting. Was he really that transparent? He was really glad that Jonathan gave no indication regarding his sexuality. Before he could catch his breath, Jonathan started again.

After completely tearing down his life, Jonathan began to point out all the good qualities he saw. He explained how he knew Michael was talented, kind and considerate and always tried to be honest and helpful toward others. He also pointed out that Michael had always been unhappy with his own physical attributes.

Finally, Jonathan ended with a last comment, "I can tell you're a very special man. As for any major relationship, I think you'll eventually find exactly what you're looking for. It might be closer than you think. And remember this. There are some out here who are looking for someone just your size and with all your qualities. Trust me. And that person will give you all the love and care you seek." He paused for a moment, "There's something else I want to tell you. What you did at breakfast. That was very considerate of you, thanking Max. Not many would take the time or even think about doing it. It shows how kind and considerate you are. I find that a very great quality in a person."

There were several moments of silence before Michael finally spoke, "Damn! Wow! What can I say? Geez! Okay! You're really good at this. To be honest, do I dare tell you? You hit all the nails right on the head. Yeah. All of them. Damn! Wow!" He shook his head. "Wow! Damn!" He gave a nervous chuckle. After a moment, he looked right at Jonathan. "And I didn't mind telling Max. I believe folks should be praised where it is deserved. So many times people hear the complaints but they never hear the good. I don't think that's fair. People need to hear the good. I believe it helps them become a better person and it builds their self-esteem."

Jonathan added, "I believe the same thing. Praise should be given where it is deserved. People need that. You're absolutely correct. Now, it's your turn. Do you want to tell me what you see and know about me? I'm ready. Tell me." He looked right at Michael and grinned, "And don't hold anything back. Be honest. I've lived long enough to get a hard-shell about things."

"All right. If you insist." Again, there was a long pause before Michael started. He looked right at Jonathan. "First off, I see an extremely confident man. Self-assured. Sophisticated. Extremely well mannered. Happy with himself and his physicalness. I see a man of money, fine things, high social status but he doesn't let it all go to his head. You seem to be grounded and have always had a plan for your life. I believe your ability to read people has made you a wealthy man as well as one who plays his cards close to his vest when it comes to important things. I think you're straightforward with everyone and honest where it truly matters. I don't see you as someone who has had any significant relationships. I don't think you've had the time much less found someone who turns your head. Now, don't get me wrong. I believe you know exactly what you're looking for. If you found it, you possibly would've made a move. But not real sure on that." Michael paused for a moment, giggled, shaking his head, "And on top of all that, you are one incredibly handsome, handsome man."

Jonathan smiled, "Well, thank you very much. Interesting. Very interesting. Very good. I will say you're correct except on one thing. I definitely would be a bit hesitant to make that move you mentioned. I do have some fears." Jonathan nodded his head. "Now, would you like to know more?" He looked at Michael and could see the silent affirmative.

"I was born illegitimate." He looked out at the waterfall. "There were stories about who was my real father. It was rumored he was a big banker in Switzerland. Married. I found out he set up a very large trust for me. Enabled me to get the finest education. Took very good care of my mother. They loved each other so much, they dared to have another child. My brother, Paul. She told me I could never try to find out who my father really was as it would be very explosive in social circles. I know she truly loved him and I know now, he truly loved her. I also know I wouldn't be in the position I am in right now, without the help and guidance of a man with whom I became very close. I didn't know it at the time but he actually was my father. He knew who I was but I didn't know who he was. Because of his guidance, I have done quite well in the world of finance."

"I took my mother's maiden name in order to keep the secret. She had great human qualities. I've always tried to live up to her expectations. I really miss her. She passed away twelve years ago. I've been lucky, though. There's always been Aunt Beatrice. She's a wonderful woman. I love her dearly. She has always told me the truth and what I needed to know. I respect her opinion highly. If anyone really knows me, she does. She knows me completely." There was a slight pause and then a complete change in the subject, "You'll meet her." He gave a big smile.

Michael was totally confused and surprised, "What? Meet her? I don't understand."

"There's going to be a big party in a few days to celebrate. She'll be coming down for it. You can meet her then." Jonathan stopped short, "Damn. I'm sorry. Here I'm planning your itinerary without even thinking that maybe you already have plans. Damn! I'm so sorry."

Michael clapped his hands. "Hey! I think it's great. I'd love to come to the party. I love parties. I guess it's going to be a fancy thing."

"I want you to do me one favor. Promise me on the first night, you will wear the same things you did when I first saw you last night."

Michael was ecstatic. That saved him from pondering his attire, wondering if he had something suitable. "No sweat. I can do that."

Jonathan gave a big smile, "Great! And I was serious about this summer. You can come and be my guest at the cottage."

Michael had been listening intensely to Jonathan as he described his life and things he had done. Every sentence made him realize he liked him more and more. Jonathan's ability to take control of a situation and grab the reins was a quality he'd always admired. Yet, Jonathan didn't seem to be possessive or have a jealous streak, proof of his self-assurance and self-confidence. There was one thing he was curious about that Jonathan never addressed. It was regarding his eye patch. He was going to ask but thought he would just wait until Jonathan mentioned it and was ready to talk about it.

"Okay. I have a few more places I want to show you before we head back. As I said, you might even want to paint some of them sometime. There's one in particular, I want to save for last. But I think I'll save it for another day." He turned, looking up high onto the far mountain. A warm smile and sereneness came to his face and

40

he spoke quietly, "I'm sure you'll want to paint it." He seemed to be lost for a few moments before he finally came back to reality again.

They spent the rest of the afternoon going to the other places special to Jonathan. Each place had a story to go with it and each secluded location was a living painting. Michael noticed that although these places were personal to Jonathan, none ever involved any other person of interest. At one place, the view looked out and down across the mountain lake with the hotel in the distance.

Michael expressed his mental thinking, "This looks like a travel poster for some fantastic chateau tucked away in some far wonderland."

Jonathan agreed, "Strange you should say that. Several French chateaus as well as a few cathedrals had an influence on the architectural design of the hotel."

Although the air was crisp, the sun shone brightly, allowing all the natural color and beauty of the wild landscape to show its best. Every turn in the path was another spectacular view.

Michael stopped his horse. "Jonathan, I could easily spend several lifetimes painting landscapes around here. It's like I've never seen such beautiful scenery."

"How are you at portraits?"

"I find them extremely tedious and unforgiving. Guess that's why I don't do them. Why do you ask?"

"Thought about having one done but haven't decided on who I'd like to do it. We might have to discuss it."

"With your charm, how does anyone ever say 'no' to you? But trust me. I'm not your portrait painter. Landscapes and still life paintings. Yes. But not portraits."

Jonathan gave a big smile and his right eye sparkled, "All right. If you say so. But maybe you know of a good one."

It was late afternoon when they returned to the stable to let go the horses. The stable master grabbed the reins of Jonathan's horse. "Did you have a good ride, sir?"

"Thank you, William. It was a wonderful day. Everything is so beautiful in the spring."

When they got back to the pavilion, Jonathan fixed himself and Michael a drink. "Can you stay for dinner? I'll call up to the dining room and have something brought down." He handed Michael an Old Fashioned.

"Well, I don't want to be an imposition." Michael seemed to stutter as he accepted the cocktail, "Thank you."

"If I didn't want you to stay, I wouldn't have asked. Now, what would you like?"

Michael realized he was right. He'd never have asked if he didn't want it to happen. "I'm easy. I like everything. You knew what you were doing last night when you ordered dinner for me. Go for it."

"Done." Jonathan picked up the telephone located on the bar cabinet. "Hello, Max. Michael is having dinner with me this evening. I'll leave it up to you. Surprise us. Thanks, Max." He hung up the phone.

Michael had to chuckle to himself when he saw the phone. It was obviously from a bygone era. But then, he realized that it did fit in with the antique furnishings of the house. A modern one would have looked so out of place.

Jonathan continued, "I love Max. He's a terrific man. He was the best chef in Europe and he's been the head chef at the hotel for nearly ten years. He treats me like gold and is always accommodating. I think the hotel is incredibly lucky to have such a man at the helm of the dining room and kitchen. Now, I want to take a shower and change before dinner. How about you?"

"Well, I'd like that but I have no other clothes."

"Not a problem. Check the closet and dresser in your room. See if there's anything there you might like to wear. Nothing fancy. Casual. Go take your shower and I'll get things started down here." Jonathan went to light the fire in the fireplace.

Michael went up to the bedroom, put his clothes on a chair then went to take a shower. After drying himself, he went to the closet. There was a whole wardrobe of clothes. He pulled out a shirt, holding it up to himself. "Damn. It looks like it would fit quite well." He went to the large dresser in the room. Opening the drawer, he found a pair of short pants and underclothing. He normally went 'commando' but with wearing someone else's clothes, he decided to restrain himself. Trying them on, it was as if the clothes were made for him. But how could this be? Who did they belong to? It was obvious they weren't Jonathan's. Was there someone in Jonathan's life he hadn't been told about?

Suddenly, he heard the shower in the bathroom and Jonathan calling out, "Go down and get comfortable by the fire and finish your drink! I'll be down in a few minutes!"

"All right! See you downstairs!" Michael yelled out, finished dressing and went down to the living room, "I'm going to take him up on getting comfortable." He took a pillow off the settee and stretched out on the rug in front of the fireplace.

His mind sorted through the happenings of the day and realized he was beginning to really like Jonathan. He had to admit although taken aback by his uninhibited personality, Jonathan was real. His actions and words were those of someone trying to hide nothing. He was a man who spoke his mind. His obvious money had not created some 'better than you', snob attitude. He accepted everyone as an equal and treated all with respect. One's level of income didn't appear to be an issue. "But what else is behind those intense green eyes? Wonder why he wears a patch? I'll bet there's one hell of a story concerning it."

Suddenly, he heard Jonathan's voice above and behind, "Well, I see you took me at my word about getting comfortable." He had a big smile on his face, "I'm glad. I'm glad you feel comfortable here. Mind if I join you?"

Michael gestured with his right hand. "Come on down!"

Jonathan grabbed his drink, another pillow and got down near Michael. Both were on their stomachs on the rug, in shorts, their cocktails on the marble fireplace hearth, looking into the fire. "Interesting you should choose to wear short pants, too."

At that moment, the phone rang.

"That's Max." Jonathan got up to answer it, "Hello, Max. Yes. Set it up in the living room instead of the dining room, please. Yes. Michael and I will be upstairs to be out of your way while you set things up. Thank you, Max. I really appreciate it. Oh, yes, could you bring some cracked ice, too? Thank you." He hung up the phone and walked over to Michael, extending his hand. "Let me help you up. Let's go upstairs while they set up dinner. It'll take them just a few minutes. Best to be out of their way while they do it."

Michael grabbed Jonathan's hand and stood up. He grabbed both pillows and placed them on the settee. They went upstairs and into Jonathan's bedroom.

Looking around, Michael saw a sepia photograph of a young

boy and woman. It was in an ornate gold frame on the bureau. She was a stunning woman with dark hair and dark eyes. The boy had coal-black hair. The woman was absolutely striking. It had to be his mother. She was wearing a most unusual necklace. A large, dark, emerald-cut type stone was on a heavy woven chain. It was impossible to tell what the gem was in the sepia photograph.

"She is a beauty, isn't she?" Jonathan spoke, seeing Michael staring at the picture, "That's my mother. Was taken when I was about four. Yes. And that's me with her." He pointed to another photo there. "That's me and my younger brother, Paul. I love that picture. It was taken not long before he went to Switzerland."

Michael looked at the sepia photograph of the two men. Paul was somewhat shorter than Jonathan but a very handsome man. Dark hair, beard and mustache softened his smiling face.

As Jonathan spoke, a momentary expression of sadness came to his face, "Paul was such a terrific guy. Seven years ago he was skiing in Switzerland and there was an avalanche. Paul was caught in it and was killed." He paused for a moment, staring at the floor, "He was twenty-nine. I really miss him. We were really close. I could talk to him about anything and everything and knew it wouldn't go anywhere." He looked directly at Michael. "I hope you don't mind. Those are his clothes. He was just your size. That's why I knew his clothes would fit. You don't mind, do you?"

"Oh, Jonathan. I'm so sorry about your brother. But of course not. Don't be silly. I'm honored you'd let me wear them." He looked back at the picture of Jonathan and his mother. "I see in the one of you and your mother, she's wearing a most incredible necklace."

"Yes. It's the necklace my father gave her. It is quite exceptional. Would you like to see it?"

Michael was totally shocked, "What!? You have it here!? Seriously? Oh! Wow! Yes, I would!"

Jonathan led Michael over to a set of dresser drawers and opened the top one. On the right side was a large wooden box. He took it out, placed it on the top of the dresser and opened the lid. The interior of the box was lined with a black velvet material and there were many pieces of jewelry there. Then, he pulled the top section off, revealing a lower level, divided into two sections. On the left were several pieces of jewelry, including the necklace. He picked it up and handed it to Michael.

Michael peered into the large, deep blue stone. "Holy Cow! This looks like the damn Hope Diamond." He looked at Jonathan. "Is it real?"

"Oh, yes. All thirty-four point five carats."

"Why the hell don't you have it in a vault? Geez! Someone could run off with it." His tone was rather scolding.

"Michael. I trust everyone truly close to me. I can't imagine any one of them, running off with it like you said. And it's like the money I keep here." He lifted a lid covering the right side of the compartment, showing a very large stash of bills. He then closed the lid. "There has never been a problem."

Michael couldn't tell the amount in the box as Jonathan only had the lid open a very short time but he knew it wasn't just pocket change. "Damn! You really are trusting. What can I say? I do have to chuckle, though. Anyone trying to fence such a stone would raise many eyebrows and questions. You bet."

Just then, there was a rustling noise downstairs. "Dinner has arrived." Jonathan's whole demeanor changed and he chuckled, "It should be interesting to see what Max has decided to send us." He closed up the box, placed it back in the drawer and shut it.

Michael was totally amazed at Jonathan's openness, honesty and his ability to trust. Also, his momentary look of sadness gave him a slight insight into the emotions deep inside.

Finally, the noise was gone and they went down to eat.

There was a wonderful set up in front of the fireplace. Three small tables, dressed with linens, were laid out with silver chafing dishes, china, silver flatware as well as crystal goblets for wine and water. A wine bucket, containing a bottle of white wine and ice, was on Jonathan's bar cabinet, along with a bottle of red wine. There was one other large container with cracked ice in it.

Jonathan walked over and systematically lifted the lids to check the contents of each chafing dish. There was a crystal bowl with a lid, containing a green salad. The dressing was in a cut-glass cruet. "I have to hand it to Max. Everything looks great. Hope you like the dressing for the salad. It's one Max came up with. I love it. And he knows I do. Here, get your plate and get started. I'll pour the wine." Jonathan opened the bottle of white. "I'll open the bottle of red, too, for later. Let it breathe a little first." He opened the bottle of red wine and left it on the bar cabinet. He poured glasses of white for both of them, handing one to Michael.

"Have to tell you, it really smells good." Michael took a plate and placed portions from every dish on it.

Before Jonathan prepared his plate, he stoked the fire to get a good blaze going. He then picked up his wine glass and raised it in the air. "To a newfound friend. In hopes, he remains one for a lifetime."

"Thanks, Jonathan. That is kind of you. And to you, too." Michael raised his glass. "Have to tell you, I think you're a great guy. I hope the same."

They ate, discussing the food and its excellence all through the meal. Finally, everything was eaten. There had been just enough of everything for them both.

"Would you like some more wine?" Michael spoke out.

"Please."

Michael picked up Jonathan's glass and headed for the wine bucket. He placed the goblets on the bar cabinet and picked up the wine bottle. He was not familiar with the vineyard but he did see the date. It was 1900. He couldn't believe they were drinking such an old bottle of wine. He whispered to himself, "Wonder how much this one cost? Damn." He poured the two glasses and placed the empty bottle back in the chilling bucket. He handed one glass to Jonathan then they sat on the rug near the fire. "That's the last of the white."

"Thanks. We'll start with the red with the next glass."

Michael took the lead in the conversation, "Have to tell you. I've thoroughly enjoyed the time we've shared today. I think you're a great guy. Even with your obvious money, you're laid-back and unpretentious and it hasn't jaded your perception of others. One's income level doesn't seem to have an influence on who you consider a friend. I think that's incredible."

"Why, thank you. Yes. Some think just because I have a large trust, I should not work. I think it's necessary, so one knows the problems of the working people and their condition. I think it keeps me grounded in reality. Too many of the rich live in ivory towers. And worst of all, they never listen."

"How true. How true." Michael nodded his head. "Listening

to people is, to me, one of the most essential parts of being a good manager."

"I have to admit, money can be a great thing to limit financial problems but it definitely cannot buy true friendship. And it definitely can't buy you love." Jonathan's eyes stared off into space as if thinking about or recalling some distant memory. But he quickly returned to reality.

"It's a good thing you have such an astute perception of people. I'm sure it has helped you avoid 'takers'. I've sure had my share of them. I sometimes think I have 'USE ME' written across my forehead." Michael bent his head down, pointing at it and chuckling, "One of these days. Yeah. One of these days, I just might find someone who'll share and not just take."

Jonathan agreed, "I think you will. I'm sure of it. And if I might be so bold, I must tell you. When first I saw you in the dining room, I saw a handsome man and wondered if you had a brain. Then, you came here and we started talking. I realized we could become great friends." He raised his glass. "Here's to friendship."

Michael raised his glass, too, and started to chuckle, "Funny. I, too, wondered if YOU had a brain. So many attractive men are just that and there is nothing between their ears but air."

They both couldn't help but snicker.

"By the way, the party is Wednesday night, the fourteenth. It'll probably start around eight. It should be a lot of fun. I can't wait for you to meet Aunt Beatrice. She's a 'one of a kind'. I know you're going to like her."

"So, you think my outfit will be all right?"

"Michael. It's you. I wouldn't have it any other way. And if I didn't explain it well enough, you look so nice in it. Oh. I forgot to tell you. The celebration will last through the weekend. If you want to wear something else the other nights, you can. Check out the clothes in the closet. I think Paul would be pleased you were wearing his formal attire."

"Well, thank you. By the way, who's going to be there? Besides your aunt?"

"Several of my friends. Most from New York. You'll like them. Yes. Some of them can be pretentious as hell but they're a good bunch. Just be you and they'll love you." Jonathan grinned and wiggled his eyebrows, "Unfortunately, I'll be going back with them on Monday. I have to head to Europe on the first. Business."

Michael nodded. "Hey. Business is business. Work before pleasure and all that stuff. I understand. And I have to go home anyway next Thursday, the twenty-second."

"I hope you'll take me up on my offer to come to visit this summer. I really enjoy your company."

"Before you leave on Monday, I'll give you my address and we can work out the visit. I'd like that."

Jonathan checked to make sure the fire screen was set to prevent any sparks from popping out. "Well, looks like we've eaten everything and drank all the wine. Think I'm about ready for bed."

"Yeah. Think I'll start another painting tomorrow. Some of the hotel guests have taken my card and seem to be interested in giving me commissions. Maybe I'll meet a few more tomorrow. You never know."

"Since you've painted the cottage, bring it by. I'd love to see it. I'll be busy tomorrow myself. How about coming by on Tuesday night for dinner?"

"Sounds good to me."

"Okay. See you in the morning. I'll fix some coffee when we get up."

Michael headed for the stairs. "In the morning." He called back and went up to his room.

As he lay in bed, he reminisced events with Jonathan. Then, he thought of the place Jonathan hadn't taken him yet, "I wonder where it is and why he's saving it for last? It must be very special." He also had a question as to what Jonathan meant when he said celebration. What was he celebrating? It must be significant if many of his friends and associates were coming to join in with it. He shook his head. "Just let the pieces fall as they should. All in good time. The answers will come all in good time." He rolled over and closed his eyes. Shortly, he was asleep.

CHAPTER VIII

The dim morning light was coming through the window of Michael's room when he awoke. He'd rested well. Then, he became aware of noise in the bathroom. Jonathan must be up, too. He found himself smiling at the thought. Had the short time he'd spent with Jonathan made him realize he not only enjoyed his company but Jonathan's presence brought him calmness, a comfort level he'd not known before? There was a sense of peace and tranquility in his head that was refreshing. He made the decision he hoped Jonathan would like the painting of his 'cottage' because he was going to give it to him as a gift. He still had to laugh at how Jonathan called his ornate residence a 'cottage'.

Michael got out of bed and walked to the bathroom door. He knocked. "Jonathan, I'm heading downstairs. See you in a few minutes."

"All right. Be down in a minute. Let me finish shaving first."

Finally, Jonathan came down and started the coffee on the little single burner stove located at the bar cabinet. Michael had to laugh to himself as he hadn't seen a percolator coffee pot in ages. A memory of his early years at his grandparents came to mind when the family would visit them for the Christmas holidays. He did remember it made the best coffee.

"I know it may sound ridiculous but I just can't seem to function without my coffee in the morning. Before I do anything, I have to have my coffee. Some think I'm overly obsessive about it." Jonathan snickered.

"Hey! I know exactly what you mean. I feel the same way."

Coffee done, they both readied to do what they had planned for the day. They headed for the door. Michael turned. "See you Tuesday evening. What time do you want me to drop over?"

"How about around seven? I'll have Max send something down for us. Anything special you'd like?"

"I'll leave it to you. I'm easy. Remember? Later. Later."

"Okay, cowboy. Plan to stay here until the parties are finished. Oh. And don't you go disappear on me."

Michael gave a big smile, "Don't worry. If the Fates will it, I'll be right here."

As Michael walked back to the hotel, he couldn't get the smile off his face and the happenings of the last two days. Maybe a page was turning in his life. Maybe for the better? He did have to remember that there had been no indication that Jonathan could be more than a friend. After all, Jonathan had given no definite indication that he was on the 'same side of the fence' as Michael. He didn't want to read anything into the situation. All Jonathan's congeniality could be because he was a terrific guy.

He breathed in the crisp morning air and took pleasure in all he saw. All the blooming spring flowers seemed more colorful and brighter than he remembered. It was going to be a good day.

Entering the lobby, he saw Paul at the front desk. "I cannot believe you're still here." He shook his head.

"Good morning, Mister Michael. From the sound of your voice, you seem really chipper this morning. I didn't see you leave earlier. I hope all is well."

"Paul, it's a long story but a good one." Michael gave a 'thumbs-up'. "I think my life is about to change. It could be for the better. And that's a good thing." In his mind, he still had to think that his and Jonathan's relationship would be just very good friends.

"Well, sir. I recognize that look and demeanor. Seen it lots of times." Paul winked his eye and smiled, "Have a good morning, sir." Paul waved and got back to the guest at the desk.

Michael went to his rooms, took down the landscape he'd started days earlier, leaning it against the wall and set the painting of the pavilion on his easel. He stared at it intensely. "Yes. It's done. And it's really good. Wish I had a nice frame for it. Of course!" He grabbed the keys to his car and went to the front desk. "Paul, do you know if there's a nice picture frame shop in town?"

"Why, yes. It's near the college on the main street there. As you drive in, it will be on the right-hand side of the street."

"Great! Thanks!" Michael was ecstatic. Since his canvas was a standard size, finding a wonderful frame was not out of the question.

There it was, just as Paul had indicated. He parked on the street and walked into the shop. He was totally surprised at the excellent selections.

An older gentleman walked up. "May I help you, sir?"

"Why, yes, I'm looking for a gold leaf, ornate frame for a twenty-four by thirty-six. Something with sculpted ornamental corners. It would be great if the surface was more of a brushed, antique gold look instead of a bright finish."

"I think I have what you are looking for right in the back. Come with me." He led Michael to the back of the shop where there were several rows of museum-quality frames. Just what he was seeking. The man moved several aside until he announced, "How about this one, sir?"

Michael was amazed to see a most incredible frame. It was

perfect. He was filled with joy there would be such a perfect frame. "It's perfect! That's it! Wow! I can't believe it! How lucky can I be!?"

The store clerk smiled, "I'm glad you approve, sir. Shall I wrap it up for you?"

"Yes. Yes, indeed."

He pointed. "It already has the hanger wire on the back. I'll give you several small brads, so you can keep the canvas in the frame."

"That's terrific. I have a hammer already in the trunk of the car. Now. Oh, please, tell me you take plastic."

"Yes, sir. We do."

As the man placed the brads in a small bag, Michael immediately went into his wallet and pulled out his Mastercard. He handed it to the clerk.

Returning to the hotel, Michael grabbed the frame, the small bag and the hammer from his car. He rushed through the lobby and to his rooms. He saw no one behind the front desk as they were most likely in the office. He couldn't wait to see the canvas in the frame. He laid the frame face down on the floor, carefully slipped the canvas in and tacked it in with the brads. Trying not to look, he closed his eyes as he placed it on the easel, turned and ran about ten feet away. Turning around, he opened his eyes.

It was more than he had hoped for. "Damn! Did I really paint it? What can I say!? That frame is excellent. I wonder what Paul will think?" After a short pause, he whispered, "I wonder what Jonathan will think?"

He looked at the mantel clock. It was only ten-thirty. Mid-morning. "I want to show Paul. I hope there isn't a bunch of people at the front desk."

He headed out the door with the painting, into the elevator and down to the first floor. Since there were no guests at the front desk, he rushed to some ten feet from the desk where Paul was standing. "Okay, Paul. What do you think?" He turned the painting around, so it faced Paul.

"Oh! Mister Michael! It is beautiful! Absolutely beautiful! Like Monet and Renoir mixed together. It looks like you stole it from a museum." He chuckled and clapped his hands, "You really are talented. The picture is alive with color. It seems to glow. Yes. Absolutely beautiful. And that frame really sets it off. Interesting you should choose Mister Jonathan's residence. You must present this painting to the board. I'll bet they will end up purchasing it. Trust me. And by the way, there's a wonderful place you might want to paint if you haven't discovered it already. It's way back in the gardens toward the mountains. It is high up and it looks out and over the entire area. I believe you're one of the few who could do it justice. A small chapel. Here, let me draw you a quick map, so you can find it. It's rather out of the way and not many go there because it is so secluded." Paul drew a quick sketch of a map and handed it to Michael.

"Thank you. You're way too kind about my work. And the chapel. I'll check it out. I'm about ready to start another canvas."

"If you do paint it, I definitely want to see it. With what you did with Mister Jonathan's residence, I know it will be a truly beautiful picture."

Martin heard Paul and came out of the office to see what he was talking about and saw the painting. "Mister Michael, well done. It is a beautiful painting."

"Thank you, Martin. I appreciate that." Michael looked at Paul.

"Well, to change the subject, what have you been doing today? You look a little distraught."

Paul shook his head. "Oh! It's my taxes. In a few days, it will be the fifteenth and they're due. Been working on them for several days and what a pain. Looks like I'll get some money back but it's the hassle of just doing them. I have a man who does them for me but it's the gathering of all the stuff together and separating it all out. I don't know why I always wait till the last minute."

"Yes, I know. I got mine done a few weeks before coming on my trip. And you know, I think there is an irony about tax day being April fifteenth. You do realize, it's the same day the Titanic sank. I believe the date was chosen with that in mind. A governmental joke on the populace. It's the day everyone gets that 'sinking' feeling." He smiled as he chuckled.

Paul responded, "Strangely enough, business will pick up again after the fifteenth. It always does. I think it's the sign of relief, everyone has survived that day." He then changed the subject back to Michael's painting, "Your painting is wonderful. We may need to get you back here in the summer and have a showing for you. I'll bet your paintings will sell very quickly as good as you are."

"Thank you, Paul, for the encouragement. We shall see about this summer. It just might happen."

Michael returned the painting to his rooms, placing it on the easel. He looked down at the one leaning against the wall. All that one needed was a few more touches of paint and it would be done. He gathered up another canvas and his paints to go start another one. This would be his third. He would put the finishing touches on the second one at a later time.

He followed the map sketch Paul had given him. Along the way, he discovered a part of the garden, containing a beautiful fountain and a wide graceful stone staircase. He knew this would have to be another painting. The scene reminded him of an incredibly beautiful Thomas Kinkade painting he had seen in an art gallery in Saint Augustine, Florida.

Finally, he arrived. There it was. A beautiful, small, Gothic-style chapel. The perfect spot to paint it would show the chapel, the mountain vista behind it and the lake in the valley below. He quickly set up his easel and readied to paint. But first, he was curious about the chapel. He went over and tried to open the door but it was locked shut. He thought it strange the chapel would be locked, especially since Jonathan didn't lock his house. He'd have to ask Paul about it. But he knew he had to get busy. There was so much intricate detail work on the delicate and lacy building. It was going to take some time to capture it with paint.

By late afternoon, he had much of the new canvas covered with the basic layout and foundation colors. He worked on it again into the mid-afternoon on Tuesday. He thought he could finish it in one more day. Now, he had to get back to the room to get ready to go to Jonathan's for dinner.

Before heading to his rooms, he went to the entry to the dining room and asked the host if he could have several lengths of butcher paper from the kitchen. He wanted to wrap the painting with them. He used his outstretched arms to show him how long. The young man at the main desk was kind enough to get them for him as Michael did not want to interrupt Max, knowing he was most likely very busy with getting things ready for dinner that night.

He stopped by the front desk and asked Martin if he could have several pieces of adhesive tape to secure the paper around the painting. Martin gave him a roll and told him to return it when he was done. Then, it was off to his rooms where he wrapped the painting, securing it with strips of tape. He was very careful not to let the paper hit the painting as the paint was still not dry. He quickly ran down and returned the tape. "Thank you, Martin. I do appreciate it."

Returning to his rooms, he decided to take a rest after prepping his clothes for the evening along with the outfit for the party on Wednesday night. He tried to imagine how the next few days would unfold. From the way Jonathan described it, it was going to be a constant party until he and all his guests left the next Monday morning. It sounded so exciting.

CHAPTER IX

It was almost a quarter to seven as he passed through the lobby. He had his clothes over one arm, black cowboy hat stacked on top of the brown one on his head. His black boots were under his other arm, holding the painting of the pavilion. A tube of newly opened toothpaste and his razor were in his pocket. He didn't see Paul at the desk. "Maybe he got some time off." That made him chuckle as he headed out the side door and down the pathways and stone stairs along the way. He would be at Jonathan's in time.

Jonathan was standing in the doorway in anticipation of Michael's arrival. "You did make it. The Fates are kind and didn't take you away from me." He saw Michael had his hands full. "Here. Let me help you. What did you bring anyway?" He took the black hat from atop Michael's brown one and placed it on his own head.

"Just my clothes and stuff to wear for tomorrow night's dinner. And something for you. But you can't see it till Sunday night." He looked up at Jonathan, wearing his cowboy hat set back on his head. "Hey. You look damn good in a cowboy hat. Yeah. Yippy-ki-yo-ki-ya."

"Thank you." Jonathan grabbed some of Michael's clothes as they walked into the living room. "I don't know if I can wait that long. Why do I have to wait till Sunday night?"

"The parties will be over and you'll be going out of town and I'll be going home on Thursday. It's my goodbye gift to you."

"Hey. What's this 'goodbye' stuff? Call it an 'I'll see you later' gift. Do you think you're just going to waltz into my life, become a friend then waltz out of it and disappear? Hell no!" Jonathan was adamant.

Michael was so pleased Jonathan liked him. The feeling was mutual. "Okay. It can be an 'I'll see you later' gift." He took the painting and leaned it against the leg of the piano. Yes, he did hear Jonathan say 'become a friend', so he had to not let himself think something more significant.

"Hope you're hungry. Max is sending dinner down in about an hour. We can have a drink before it gets here. Let's get your things up to your room first."

Michael heard Jonathan. There it was again. Was it just a slip of the tongue or was there something intentional to it when he said 'your room' and not 'Paul's room'? He shook his head as if trying to remove some reluctant cobwebs there. He didn't want to read anything into the comment.

After putting Michael's things upstairs, they were back in the living room with Jonathan making drinks. "So, what did you do all day yesterday and today?"

"Started my third painting. I think I'll be able to finish it with one more full day of work."

"Three paintings? Humm." He paused for a few seconds, "I think I know what your gift is." He looked toward the piano and the wrapped rectangular object leaning against it. "Does it have a building in it?" He gave a sly snicker.

"You weren't supposed to guess. It was supposed to be a surprise." He started to giggle as if no one could have figured out what the gift was. He was an artist and the shape of the gift was telltale. It didn't take a rocket scientist to guess what was under the butcher paper.

"It will be. And I'm sure it will be a very nice surprise." Jonathan changed the subject, "Do you have plans for tomorrow during the day? If not, I had thought we could go riding some more. I know I'm taking away from your time you would be painting. So, if you need to paint, I definitely understand."

"Hey! I can always paint. I'd love to go riding tomorrow. I truly enjoy spending time with you."

"Great. I'll have Max fix us up a basket for lunch to take with us."

It was going on eleven o'clock and they were settled in by the fire, continuing their conversation.

Michael commented, "I swear, one of these days, I want to take a long tour of Europe and see some of the museums there. All that art. All in one place. It would be fantastic. I'm sure you have been to many of them, having traveled there."

Jonathan responded, "Yes, you're right. There's nothing like seeing art up close and in person. I bought many paintings to hang here by unknown artists. I bought them because I like them. I have no idea if any of the artists will become famous." He laughed, "But to me, that doesn't matter. Regardless of the artist or the painting's commercial value, what matters is how I like it. THAT is where its true value comes in for me."

Michael agreed, "You did the right thing. I always tell people to buy a painting because they like it. If it becomes valuable down the road, so be it."

"Hey. Maybe you'll become famous one of these days!" Jonathan smiled.

"Yeah. Sure." Michael snickered, "As my mother would say, 'Don't hold your breath. You'd look like hell blue!'"

"Well. Here's to art." Jonathan raised his drink.

"Sure. To art." Michael raised his glass.

"And speaking of art, you should see the paintings Aunt Beatrice has. They are very nice."

They continued talking into the early morning before heading up to bed. Michael brought out the tube of toothpaste for Jonathan to try. They both brushed their teeth.

Jonathan loved the new paste. "I'll have to find some of this at the store. It's much creamier and smoother than the powder I have."

"You can say that again." Michael snickered.

The next day, they spent riding on the trails and touching on stories of their lives. Michael came to see more and more of Jonathan's personality. He spoke of many people he knew but none seemed to be really super close friends. The exceptions were Max and his favorite aunt.

Jonathan clapped his hands and shook his head when he mentioned that if anyone knew him, it was his aunt. From his stories, most of the people he knew were in New York. It made sense. His aunt lived there and his major finance work was there. While in New York, he obviously mingled with and came to know the people there. And of course, many were business associates and clients.

When they returned to the pavilion, they began to get ready for the party that night. It was going to be in the hotel dining room as would be the subsequent parties. Jonathan indicated he was expecting around thirty to come in for the celebration. It should be a lot of fun. There would be food, music and dancing for the next four days. Daily events were also planned. There would be horseback riding, boating, games, luncheons, as well as free times for the guests to do what they wanted.

Michael hoped he didn't feel like an alien or appear to be awkward. He so wanted to give a good impression for Jonathan's sake. There still had been no indication as to what the celebration was all about. Maybe something would be said while it was happening. He didn't want to press the issue.

Finally, they were dressed and ready to go up to the hotel. The first party was to begin around eight that evening, starting with dinner and dancing. Michael was nervous as hell. "Damn. You'd think it was the first formal affair I'd ever been to and didn't know how to act." He put on his black cowboy hat and looked over at Jonathan. "I have to tell you. You look marvelous in your white tie and tails. Are you sure I'm going to look all right?"

"Trust me. You're going to be the hit of the party. They're going to love you. Just be… YOU."

The night air was warmer than usual. As they got closer to the large stone terrace off the dining room, Michael saw several of the French doors were open to the terrace and the music within lilted out into the night. He could hear a piano enhanced with orchestral instruments just like on the night he first saw Jonathan.

Entering the dining room through one of the open doors, he could see there were many more than thirty people. Obviously, many of the hotel guests were having dinner, too. Across the room was a long table, decorated with flowers and candelabra and set with many place settings. That must be the table for Jonathan's guests. His mind whirled to capture everything in sight. To say, he was nervous as hell, would be putting it mildly. A total understatement.

Many guests saw them enter the room and came over, expressing their 'hello's and greetings. Regarding Jonathan's guests, it was obvious everyone knew everyone as only first names were spoken.

Michael was so aware of the looks up and down when he was introduced. Again, only first names were used. It took a little while but he finally realized Jonathan's friends were really very nice and very personable. He looked around the room, trying to pick out Jonathan's aunt but no one seemed to stand out. He was sure if she had been there, they would have greeted her first.

As one of the waiters came by, asking if they wanted something to drink, Michael asked for an Old Fashioned. The waiter looked at Jonathan and smiled, "Mister Jonathan, I already know your drink." He bowed slightly, turned and walked away.

Michael turned to Jonathan and spoke quietly, "Your aunt is not here. Did she not make it?"

"Oh. She's not here... yet. She's always the last one to arrive. Don't worry. You'll know her when you see her." He bent his head down and gave a little chuckle.

Jonathan mingled through the group, introducing Michael and engaging in conversations about Michael and how he was an artist. This seemed to be a point of extreme interest to everyone since it was so far removed from the industrial, railroading and banking occupations of the other men in the room. Michael was aware of their occupations from talking with Jonathan. After a while, he leaned over to Michael and spoke quietly, "It should be just about time."

"Just about time?" Michael looked puzzled.

Jonathan nodded. "For Aunt Beatrice to arrive."

Virtually, at that moment, an extremely elegant, older, white-haired woman with striking features, appeared, standing at the entrance to the dining room. Jonathan quickly turned to Michael. "Here she is. Be back in a minute." He headed toward the lady.

Everyone in the room seemed to stop what they were doing and all conversation ceased. The musicians also quickly ended their playing. The room was silent. All turned toward the entrance to the dining room.

To Michael, she looked like some European royalty, a little shorter than himself, wearing a long elegant white gown, long white gloves, and an elegant jeweled necklace and tiara. He saw Jonathan bow and kiss her hand, then speak softly to her. She grabbed Jonathan's face, pulled it down toward hers and gently kissed him on the lips. She turned and smiled, looking directly at Michael. They started walking in his direction. She walked as if she floated across the floor on air. As they passed, those to her sides bowed and curtsied with quiet voices, "Good evening, Lady Stanenberg." It was the first time a last name had been spoken. Michael now knew her last name. Shortly, they stood in front of him.

"Aunt Beatrice. This… is Michael." Jonathan gestured in Michael's direction.

"Hello, Michael." She spoke quietly but directly as she slowly looked at Michael, starting at his feet all the way to the top of his head. Then, she smiled and extended her hand. He now saw those bright and shining green eyes ran in the family.

Michael heard an accent in her voice. Maybe it was German or Russian. He couldn't tell. He took her hand, clicked his boot heels together, bowed slightly then looked right at her. "Nice to meet you, Madame."

"I look forward to talking with you." She smiled kindly and her eyes sparkled, "Let me go pay my respects to Jonathan's other guests." She turned to Jonathan. "My dear, do not be fussy. I can well take care of myself. You stay here and take care of your cowboy and make him feel comfortable." She looked back at Michael, smiled and winked her left eye.

Jonathan smiled, "Yes, Ma'am."

She crossed the room, extending greetings to the other guests, all of whom seemed to know her well. The men were bowing, kissing her glove-covered hand and the women giving her a curtsy and taking her hand in a slight shake.

"Wow!" Michael whispered to Jonathan, "She is so elegant and striking... and... and... so intimidating. I feel like I just met the queen."

Jonathan chuckled softly, "Yes. She can seem that way but wait till you get to know her a little. You'll see she's quite down to earth and very real. And you'll know very quickly if she likes you or not. There's no mistaking it. But don't worry. I know she's going to adore you."

At that moment, the waiter arrived with Michael and Jonathan's drinks. As they took them, Michael held his glass to Jonathan and smiled, "Here's to it, my friend. I hope I make it."

Jonathan clinked his glass to Michael's. "You're going to do just fine. Don't worry." He turned and politely asked the waiter to get his aunt a cocktail.

The waiter bowed slightly. "Immediately, Mister Jonathan. I know what she likes."

As the evening progressed, Michael felt more and more comfortable with everyone. After discovering he was a painter, they were all interested in seeing some of his artwork. The only painting that was framed and ready to be seen was the one he was giving to Jonathan and it wasn't to be opened until Sunday. Strangely, through the entire evening, he hadn't had any time to talk with Jonathan's aunt. But he knew there would be time, during the next few days.

Around midnight after the musician's last selection, everyone applauded them in appreciation of their excellence. All of the hotel guests had already left the dining room. Jonathan extended his gratitude to the musicians, giving each and every one a handsome gratuity then returned to the table where all his guests were still seated.

Jonathan took a fork and rang his water goblet. "First of all, I want to thank all of you for coming to the celebration. There's a lot planned for the next few days as you can see on the itinerary sent to everyone. I know you all are tired from your trips. So, we will meet tomorrow morning around ten down at the lake for boating. Sleep well and see you then."

Before leaving, Jonathan's aunt came up to Michael and spoke in a calm and clear voice, "It was nice to meet you, Michael."

Michael bowed slightly, clicked his heels and took her hand and kissed it. He looked at her and smiled, "It was nice meeting you, too, Madame."

Jonathan led his aunt to the entrance of the dining room, bowed, kissed her hand then gave her a hug. She kissed him gently on the lips. He waited till she had gone then returned to Michael.

Quiet 'goodbye's and 'see you in the morning's were exchanged as the group broke up and left the dining room. All expressed how much they were glad to meet Michael.

Michael watched Jonathan go to each of the waiters, thanking them and placing something in each one's hand. Lastly, he went to Max, still standing with a great smile on his face. He shook his hand.

"Job well done, Max. Job well done. Thank you. I am constantly in your debt."

Max bowed slightly. "You're so welcome, Mister Jonathan. I'm so glad you are pleased. Have a good evening, sir. See you tomorrow." He looked over at Michael. "Good evening, Mister Michael. I'm so glad you were here. See you tomorrow." He bowed again.

Michael bowed slightly. "Good evening, Max. You did a superb job. What can I say? Thank you."

Jonathan and Michael left through the French doors and headed to the pavilion.

As they entered the house, Jonathan spoke out, "So. What do you think of my friends?"

Michael stammered a bit, "Well. After I got to talk with them, I realized they are pretty nice folks. You know, I have no idea what any of their last names are. But it doesn't matter. I probably wouldn't remember them anyway." He shook his head. "Sorry, I didn't get the chance to talk with your aunt."

"Don't worry. She's the one who will choose the time she wants to talk with you. You'll get the chance, trust me." He bent his head down, shaking it. "Well, I think we should head to bed. This is just the beginning."

Michael agreed, "I am bushed. I had no idea tonight was going to be so exhausting. And I say that in a kind way. I really did have a great time."

They shared the bathroom as each took a shower and readied for bed. Michael was the first starting to leave the bathroom. "Goodnight. Call me when you're getting up. And thank you so much for inviting me. I had a wonderful time."

"Michael." Jonathan paused a moment, "I know you said you

wanted me to wait till Sunday to see the painting but I'd very much like you to share it with everyone tomorrow evening at dinner. Several, I know, are interested in seeing how good an artist you really are. I am, too. And you never know, you might get some immediate commissions." A big smile came to his face.

"If you really want to see it sooner, then you shall. You can see it right now if you like."

Jonathan was ecstatic, "Really? You wouldn't mind?"

"The painting is yours. You may see it whenever you like."

A huge grin covered Jonathan's face, "Let's go!"

They headed downstairs. Jonathan, running like some child, running down on Christmas morning to see his presents under the tree. He raced over to the painting.

"Be careful as the paint is still wet. Oils don't dry overnight." Michael giggled.

Jonathan carefully unwrapped the gift, making sure he did not let anything touch the surface of the canvas but not wanting to see it immediately. "Please, take it and put it out from me, so I can see it from a distance. I'll close my eyes first. You can tell me when to open them." Jonathan put his hands over his eyes, even the one with the patch.

"All right." Michael was getting a big charge out of watching Jonathan. He was seeing a part of him he had no idea existed. He was seeing the child within which he thought was wonderful. It made Jonathan that much more human and real. He carried the painting some ten feet from Jonathan. The light in the room was perfect. He held it up and turned the painting to face Jonathan. "Okay. You may look now."

Jonathan tilted his head back, pulled away his hands and opened his eyes. He wanted to make sure his good eye would be focused enough to see the painting immediately when he looked at it. He slowly moved his head down and gazed at the canvas. He gave a slight gasp of surprise, "Michael! It is magnificent! I love it! It's absolutely beautiful! What color and depth. It's like I could walk into it." He looked right at Michael. "And you're giving this to me? But Michael. You can't do that. It's too much."

"If I didn't want you to have it, I wouldn't have given it to you. I want to give you something important. Something of me. You've been so kind to me with all you've done. I want to show you how much I appreciate your kindness and generosity. Please. I insist."

Jonathan walked closer to the painting, looked down at it then back at Michael. He smiled, "You forgot to do something."

Michael looked questioningly at Jonathan, "What?"

Jonathan chuckled, "You forgot to sign and date it."

Michael looked at the painting. "Oh, my God. I did, didn't I? Geez. I guess I was in such a hurry to give it to you, I forgot. Not a problem. I'll do it another time. There's plenty of time."

Jonathan continued to stare at the painting as he spoke quietly, "I love it. Thank you so much."

Michael looked closely at Jonathan. In the light, he could see a line reflecting on Jonathan's face. He realized it was the tracks of tears. He smiled, "I'm so glad you like it."

Jonathan spoke almost in a whisper, "I believe she is right. Yes. Yes, I do. Aunt Beatrice is right." He gave Michael a big smile and turned away so Michael wouldn't see him wipe his tears. He composed himself then cleared his throat, "Now, it's time for bed. We have a long day tomorrow. I think it'll be fun." He headed for the stairs.

Michael leaned the painting against the leg of the piano and was right behind Jonathan. "I'm so looking forward to it." Halfway up the stairs, he spoke again, "I am so glad you like the painting. That means a lot to me."

Jonathan stopped and turned around, looking down at Michael a few steps lower. "I love it. Thank you. Thank you so much. And you could never imagine what it means to me. I can't wait for Aunt Beatrice to see it. She loves good artwork. As I mentioned before, she has quite a collection of her own. I can't wait for her to see the talent you are."

Michael lay in bed and smiled with thoughts of the party, flipping in his head. He'd really had a great time. He then reflected on the comment Jonathan made regarding his aunt 'that she was right'. What did he mean? And what did he mean when he said 'this is just the beginning'? Maybe he would find out soon enough. He couldn't dwell on it. Tomorrow was going to be another busy day. He tried very hard to clear his mind and before he realized it, he was asleep.

CHAPTER X

When Michael woke, he could hear Jonathan in the bathroom. He quickly got up and yelled out, "Jonathan, good morning!"

The bathroom door opened. "Good morning to you, too." He smiled, standing there with just a towel around himself, "I think it's going to be quite cool out, so you might want to wear your jacket again."

"I thought the same thing." He had put on his jeans and flannel shirt he'd worn the day before, his brown boots and hat and his fleece jacket. "I'll meet you downstairs."

In no time at all, Jonathan appeared in a very tailored wool outfit and cap. "Hope you are up for a little boating this morning. I have to do it today. It's the fifteenth. It's my way of coping." He gave a nervous laugh and stared off into space as if recalling some memory. His right hand moved to the upper center of his chest and his fingers moved as if trying to grasp something there. "But first, let's get something to eat."

They went up the paths and stairs in the garden to the terrace and through the French doors of the hotel dining room. Jonathan called out, "Good morning, Max. And how are you this morning? Thank you so much for dinner last night. It was wonderful."

"It was my pleasure, Mister Jonathan. I'm expecting everyone down shortly to eat."

Suddenly, Michael was aware of a young child standing in the entry of the dining room. It was a boy around five or six years old. He came walking through the dining room right to Jonathan,

Michael and Max then turned to Max. "Papa, can I go see the horses for a while?" He spoke with joy in his voice.

Max responded, "Son. Where are your manners? You remember Mister Jonathan? This is his friend, Mister Michael."

The boy looked up at Jonathan and Michael. "Good morning, Mister Jonathan. And to you, too, Mister Michael."

"Are you old enough to ride the horses?" Michael smiled at the boy.

"No, sir. But I think I will be old enough soon. I like to go see them and watch them. I sometimes get to give them a little sugar or a carrot. They really are very gentle." He smiled up at Michael.

Max responded, "Yes. Just be careful and don't get in anyone's way."

The boy clapped his hands together. "Thank you, Papa. I won't." He pointed at Michael's hat. "Papa. I really like his hat. Maybe I can get one like that one day?"

Michael removed his hat and when he placed it on the child's head, the hat came down over his eyes and everyone laughed, "I think you'll have to get a little bit bigger before you can wear one of these. And when you do, I'll bet you'll be big enough to ride horses."

The boy giggled and handed Michael his hat back, "One of these days, Mister Michael, then you and I can go riding. It was nice to have met you. It was nice to see you again, too, Mister Jonathan." He turned and was out the door in an instant.

Slowly, some of Jonathan's guests began to arrive and were seated at various tables in the dining room. Other hotel guests were also coming and going. Waves and greetings were exchanged across the room. Jonathan's aunt was nowhere to be seen.

After eating, they headed to the lake and down to the boats.

"Hope you like a little exercise. Rowing will definitely give your arms a workout." Jonathan, again, laughed nervously and brushed the center of his chest, "But it's better than swimming in the cold water."

For several hours, they rowed out and up the lake until it was around one in the afternoon. Michael sensed that Jonathan's mind seemed to be preoccupied, so there was little conversation. Jonathan headed the boat back as there was to be a late luncheon on the landing. Lawn chairs and blankets had been provided. The air was crisp but not uncomfortably cold.

Most all of the men sat on the blankets and the ladies sat in the chairs. The ladies wore long dresses and light long coats with hats to ward off the slightly cool air. Michael kept looking at everyone's attire, thinking it seemed a little strange. But not having traveled in the high upper class, he wasn't quite sure how the wealthy dressed for such events.

Jonathan's aunt arrived and was dressed very elegantly and sat in a rather prime spot. All the other women were around her as if she was the queen bee. Again, Michael didn't get the chance to talk with her. Maybe the chance would come that evening at dinner.

The rest of the afternoon was spent on the upper lawns with everyone playing croquet. It was great fun for Michael. He hadn't played in years and wasn't as good as the others. He was sure they probably played it on a regular basis. When his ball got hit and knocked halfway across the lawn, he didn't mind and just laughed out loud, clapping his hands. Everyone was pleased he was taking it so cheerfully. As the game progressed and it would come time for Michael's ball to be knocked away again, the one hitting it became quite apologetic about it and seemed to hit it reluctantly. They could see Michael was a really good sport about it all, endearing him to them even more.

Jonathan was so pleased his friends liked Michael. He knew his aunt was watching and would have much to say down the road. Of that, he was sure.

The games over, everyone began to head to the hotel to get ready for dinner. It was almost six o'clock when Michael and Jonathan headed to the pavilion.

"Jonathan, I know you said I could wear some of Paul's formal attire tonight. Are you sure you really don't mind?"

"Please. Paul's clothes seem to fit you so well. But wear your black boots and hat. I can't imagine you without them."

"Yeah. And my boots make me a little taller, too." He giggled, "Even with them on, you're over half a foot taller than me."

He looked right at Michael. "Hey. I like you just the way you are."

Michael went through the closet and found several sets of formal evening wear. He was amazed and had to laugh to himself when he put on the clothes. Paul's clothes fit him incredibly well. Fully dressed, he almost didn't recognize the man looking back from the mirror on the door. "Damn. I don't look half bad. Looks like I have money." He started to snicker loudly, "This damn tie. I hate to admit to Jonathan I've never tied one of these before. I hate to show him what a bumpkin I am."

At that moment, there was a knock at the bedroom door.

"Come in."

Jonathan entered the room and saw Michael standing there. "You look great. I still can't believe Paul's clothes fit you so well. He would be very pleased to know that such a fine man is wearing them."

"That was so nice and kind of you to say. Thank you. But. Ah. I must be honest with you. I have never tied one of these ties. You seem to have it down pat. Would you mind? I noticed Paul didn't have any of the 'clip-on' kind."

"'Clip-on' kind?" Jonathan's face expressed a questioning look, "Here. Let me do it for you." Virtually in an instant, Jonathan had the tie done perfectly. He placed his hands on Michael's shoulders, looked at the tie then smiled at Michael, "You look terrific. Wow. But let's get moving. It's almost eight. And we're bringing the painting. I want it set up before anyone gets there. I can't wait for everyone to see what an exceptional artist you are. You carry it, so nothing accidentally hits the canvas."

They headed downstairs and out the front door. In minutes, they entered the dining room and went over to the long table Max had set up again. Jonathan saw Max and immediately went over to him. "Do we have something we can put this painting on, so everyone can see it?"

"Certainly, Mister Jonathan. We'll get a display easel from the storage room." Max directed one of his staff who within minutes returned with a substantial easel on which to show off the painting.

Jonathan placed it on the easel in a spot that was well-lighted and could be seen by all in the dining room, yet out of the way enough, so no one could rub against it and smear the paint. Jonathan stood back to make sure the presentation was satisfactory.

At the same time, Max came up with a large sturdy piece of paper on a hook. He moved two chairs in front of the easel and hung the sign on the back of one. It read: 'Painting Wet. Do Not Touch!'

Jonathan and Michael saw it and came up to Max, standing

there looking at the sign. Jonathan patted Max on the shoulder, "Thank you, Max. Perfect."

Max responded, "No need to take any chances with such a beautiful painting. Well done, Mister Michael. Well done."

Michael smiled, "Thank you very much, Max."

Max bowed slightly and headed to the kitchen.

Almost immediately, hotel guests were coming up, inquiring about the painting and remarking how beautiful it was. Jonathan was very pleased everyone saw the beauty he did.

Michael was mobbed when the guests realized he was the artist. Many were asking about possible commissions.

It was wonderful to see Michael as the center of attention. Shortly, many of Jonathan's guests were entering the dining room. He knew Michael could take care of himself, so he went to greet his friends and lead them to the large table where they would be sitting. He also invited all of them to see the painting.

Everyone had arrived by the time Jonathan's aunt appeared at the entry. Again, Jonathan went to meet her and lead her to her spot at the head of the table. Everyone stood up as she arrived. "Please, come and see the painting Michael did for me. I think you'll be surprised." They walked over to the painting.

"He is very good. I like the colors and the perspective. I could almost walk into the scene." She spoke very deliberately, yet quietly.

Jonathan smiled, "I told him the same thing." He was happy with her response.

Finally, all were seated, Jonathan's aunt at the head of the table and Jonathan at the other end. Michael sat to his right. Dinner began as did the buzz of conversations mainly about Michael and his painting.

Michael realized even though he'd talked with many of Jonathan's friends, he still really didn't know anything about them. He'd some idea they were in upper management or owners of industrial companies, railroading or the banking arena but that was about it. All the women seemed to be stay-at-home wives but entertained each other often with coffees, teas, cards and other social games. The one thing he did know is they were all very, very wealthy.

Dinner over, all retired for the night. Jonathan, again, gave handsome gratuities to all the musicians and service people, thanking them profusely for their excellence. He told Michael to get the painting and they returned to the pavilion. Jonathan fixed them both a last cocktail as Michael leaned the painting up against the piano leg.

Michael spoke, "I really do like all your friends. They're a bit distant but they're so nice. Even in the strata of society where they exist, they're truly genuine folks. And they don't seem to care that I don't have a golden spoon in my mouth." He grinned.

"I knew they were going to like you. How could they not? And I believe they see how much I like you."

"But, you know. I haven't had a chance to talk with your aunt yet. I know she's watching me. I've seen her looking at me when I was least expecting it. I feel like she's gathering some sort of ammunition to get me with."

Jonathan chuckled, "Don't worry. I think she's seeing if what I have told her and what she has told me is correct."

"You told her about me? But when?"

"Oh, before she left New York. We spoke on the phone. But don't worry. Everything I said was good." He looked at Michael, flexed his eyebrows and had a big Cheshire Cat smile on his face, "I'm sure she'll be pulling you aside, soon."

Michael bent his head down, shaking it. "Oh. Geez. I'm in for it, I'm sure."

They finished their drinks and headed to bed. Heading up the stairs, Jonathan grabbed Michael who was ahead of him. Michael stopped and turned, looking at Jonathan. Jonathan spoke quietly, "Thank you so much for the painting of the cottage. It is so beautiful. I'll hang it when I get back from my trip. I'm so glad everyone got to see it. I knew they'd be appreciative and see the talent you are."

"It makes me happy you like it. And thank you for being so encouraging." Michael's face was filled with happiness.

As Michael lay in bed, he thought about his rooms in the hotel. He hoped they didn't think something was wrong, having not slept in the bed these past few nights. But he didn't care. He was having the time of his life. He knew he was going to have another long talk with Paul when he got back. He knew Paul wouldn't mind listening and wouldn't be judgmental.

CHAPTER XI

Friday was spent with horseback riding. It was interesting to Michael that Jonathan, leading the group, took them everywhere but never to any of the special places he had been shown. Michael said nothing as he knew there had to be some reason for that not happening.

Dinner that night was just as much fun as the night before with the music and dancing. The food was exceptional as was the service. Michael was so appreciative there was such a great selection of clothes to wear in Paul's closet since he'd brought only the ones he wore that Wednesday night.

The same held true for Saturday. But Sunday was left to the guests to do whatever they wanted.

Jonathan and Michael came up to the dining room for a late breakfast, Jonathan dressed in his casual wear and Michael in his jeans, flannel shirt and boots. They greeted Max and were seated at a table near the windows. Just then, Jonathan's aunt came into the room, not dressed as formally as she had been but still elegant and stylish. Jonathan jumped up and guided her to their table, pulling out a chair for her.

"Good morning, Madame. It's nice to see you again." Michael had quickly stood up, bowed slightly then sat down again after Jonathan's aunt was seated.

"Good morning, Michael." She smiled.

Jonathan returned to the table after asking Max to include his aunt.

They enjoyed small talk as they ate. The waiter cleared all the plates, leaving the coffee china. Suddenly, Michael felt Jonathan's foot bump up against his. He looked over at Jonathan with a questioning look.

Jonathan smiled back, "Michael, I have a few things I have to prepare before I leave tomorrow. Would you mind staying here with Aunt Beatrice? I'm sure she would appreciate the company."

Instantly, Michael realized that THIS was the moment. THIS was the time that Jonathan's aunt was going to talk with him. His stress level soared into orbit. He so wanted to scream out, "YOU BITCH!" for not warning him in advance but he didn't He wondered if the feeling he was having was a heart attack. He knew it was evident when Jonathan looked inquisitively at him, seeing his face blush. He smiled at Jonathan and spoke nervously, "I think that would be wonderful. Please, go right ahead. Come back when you're finished." He had a feeling this conversation was not going to be some short walk in the park.

Jonathan got up and bowed slightly to his aunt. "It's going on eleven-thirty. See you both around two. Then, we can all go get some rest before tonight's dinner."

Beatrice and Michael watched him go out the doors, across the terrace and disappear down the path to the pavilion.

Michael and Beatrice sat across the table from one another for a few moments in silence, sipping their coffee. Their waiter came by and brought a new pot, placing it in the center of the table with more cream and sugar, in fresh china containers. Michael picked up the pot and stood up. "May I?"

"Please. Thank you, Michael." Beatrice smiled at his attentiveness. After a slight moment of silence, she spoke again, "So. Michael. I have heard good things about you. You must tell me more about yourself."

It had begun. Michael knew he'd have to tell the basics of his life and place all cards on the table. Beatrice did not seem to be the kind of person from whom you could hide anything. It seemed she could see into your very soul without you saying a word. And so, he began. For around an hour and a half, he told of his history. He watched Beatrice's face as he spoke and was surprised, yet pleased, his obvious lack of money didn't have any impression on her at all. He had touched on earlier relationships he'd had, not indicating gender or names and how each one ended as they hadn't begun on a firm foundation. He was showing his inner self when he indicated how it had been easy for others to take advantage of him. He knew it was a fault but he was not apologetic for it. He had remembered an expression he once heard, 'Show me a man who is a lover and I'll show you a man with lots of scars.'

After some moments of silence, Beatrice spoke softly, "I see you have had your trials and tribulations in life. And that's not a bad thing. It can build character. And you seem to be a very good and kind man and have weathered the storms. You have only known Jonathan for a short time. Yet, I can tell you like him. And you gave him a wonderful work of art." She paused for a moment, "What do you think of my Jonathan?"

Michael described all he knew and had observed, "But every day I learn more about him. He never ceases to surprise me."

"Let me tell you about Jonathan." For almost an hour, she covered his upbringing and his rise to success in business but this was covered rather quickly as it didn't seem to be the object of the conversation. It was when she started talking about Jonathan's inner person and his emotional life, the conversation became more pointed.

She described there were a few times Jonathan had attempted a relationship, mentioning the names of several women, "But he finally realized he was not being honest with himself." Beatrice looked very hard into Michael's eyes. "I have a sense you can understand why Jonathan's relationships with women did not work out." She was silent, sipping her coffee.

It was obvious she knew the kind of man Michael was inside. She knew completely who he was.

Beatrice continued, "Jonathan has always wanted love and to be loved in the way he wants and he should have it. I have watched him struggle with himself over the years and finally talked with him. Jonathan is more special to me than you can imagine. Never have I met anyone who I believed could and would love him the way he deserves." She paused for a moment, "Not until… now." She looked right at Michael. "Michael. I see the kind and giving man you are. I see how sensitive and attentive you are with Jonathan. I believe, deep inside you, there is something building for him but you're afraid to say something. Afraid you're not good enough and rich enough. Jonathan doesn't care about money. He cares about the person. From talks I've had with him on the phone and watching him interact with you, I see he truly cares about you. If you have feelings for him and I believe you do, tell him. He's just waiting. Yes. He's aggressive and seemingly overwhelming but give him the chance and you will see a man who can deliver the emotional and physical love anyone would desire and seek in life. This is the only area of his life where he is unsure of himself."

Michael was bowled over. He was amazed. She had read him up

one side and down the other. She didn't skip a beat. She had peeled back all the segments of the artichoke and got right to the heart of the matter. She also confirmed what he had thought all along about Jonathan but wasn't totally sure and had been somewhat afraid to address it. He looked directly at her. "I don't know what to say. You've seen everything with crystal clarity. You're absolutely correct. Wow. You're truly amazing! You also answered a question that has been running around in my mind for some time now. Thank you for that." He shook his head. "You are one shrewd lady. I see why Jonathan loves you and trusts you explicitly. You are honest, straightforward and I hope you don't mind me saying this but you don't pull any punches. You tell it like it is. He said you did. Now, I completely understand. And truthfully, I like that in a person. It shows that person really loves you as well."

"Michael, if you do have feelings for him and I know you do, then tell him. You will not be sorry. I believe both of you together could move the world." She smiled.

He nodded, "I will. Life is too short."

"Strange you should say that. When his mother died and Paul was killed, it affected Jonathan greatly. His father's death four years ago was a release for him as his father finally declared him as his son in his will. All of this made him realize he was not granted tomorrow. And it's the strange turning of the wheels of Fate that he is still here today. He doesn't like to talk about it but it's the reason we all gather here every year at this time and celebrate. And it's why many went boating on Thursday. Yes. This is the third year we have all come together. I gave him a Saint Christopher's Medal for the occasion the first year. I had the Pope bless it."

"That must be the medallion he wears around his neck. The Saint of Travel."

"Yes. He said he would never take it off." She smiled, "I pray it will keep him safe for the rest of his life."

Michael was dying to ask what it was all about but could see from the expression on Beatrice's face she didn't want to discuss it as it seemed to greatly disturb her. If he wanted to know, he'd have to ask Jonathan. "Thank you so much for your candor. I definitely will talk with Jonathan. Tonight."

"Good. Do not be afraid. I know he's just waiting for you to say something. And once you have, he will take it from there. I'm happy for you. I'm happy for you both. You'll not be sorry. I like you, Michael. And I believe I will be seeing much more of you in the future." A very large smile came to her face. She reached over and grabbed Michael's right hand and squeezed it gently. Then, she spoke with a chuckle and a gleam came to her wonderful green eyes, "I see a love for artists with furry faces runs in the family." She patted Michael's hand.

Michael didn't want to question the last comment even though he was extremely curious as to what she meant. The conversation had centered around himself and Jonathan and Michael had had no time to ask Beatrice anything about her own life and history. Maybe there would be another time that would happen.

They'd gone through several pots of coffee and finally left the heavy conversation for lighter talk but this didn't last long. It was just after two o'clock. Looking out the windows, they saw Jonathan coming up the path.

Entering the room, he came over to Beatrice and took her hand, smiled and kissed her on the cheek. He looked over at Michael.

"Well, I see you survived." A huge Cheshire Cat smile filled his face and he began to laugh. Michael and Beatrice started to laugh, too. Beatrice tried to make it not so obvious by covering her mouth with her hand.

It was time they all go take a rest before getting ready for dinner. It would be the last night they'd all be together.

Beatrice ended the conversation, "Let me go. I will see you both later." Michael moved quickly to help her with the chair. "Thank you, Michael. I know I'm not wrong about you."

Michael bowed, clicked his heels and kissed her hand, "See you later, Madame."

"Michael. Call me... Aunt Beatrice." She smiled.

"Yes, Ma'am... Aunt Beatrice." He kissed her hand again.

She grabbed his face and kissed him on the cheek, turned and started off.

Jonathan led her to the entrance of the dining room and watched her as she walked away. He returned to the table as Michael was ready to leave.

Jonathan's face beamed with a huge smile, "Call me Aunt Beatrice? Call me Aunt Beatrice? Holy cow! I guess all went VERY well. And a kiss on the cheek! She seems to have taken a real liking to you. But I'm not surprised. I know she sees what I do when I look at you."

After Jonathan gave the waiter a nice gratuity, they left the dining room, heading to the pavilion.

"I have to say. She's something else. I can't believe how perceptive she is. You'd think she had a crystal ball hidden away." Michael could only shake his head.

"You have that right." Jonathan changed the subject, "Honestly, these last few days have been exhausting. Think I'll take a little nap before I get ready."

"I could go for that. You bet. Especially, after that talk with Aunt Beatrice. Wow!"

They entered the pavilion. "I'll rap on your door to wake you up. See if you can catch a few winks." Jonathan headed up the stairs.

Michael was right behind him. "See you soon."

"Oh. I'd really like it if you'd wear your original outfit again for me tonight. Do you mind?"

"Hell no! Not a problem. Be glad to."

CHAPTER XII

It was around eight o'clock when they headed up to the dining room. Jonathan had a big smile on his face, seeing Michael looking so handsome in his black outfit. Deep inside, he could feel something had been building ever since he first saw Michael. It was a good feeling. He was happier than he'd ever been.

Most of the guests were already seated when they entered the room. The music was playing and several couples were dancing. All had positioned themselves at the same places at the table established on the first night. Beatrice arrived a little late, as usual, looking absolutely ravishing. She took her place at the table.

A few minutes after Beatrice was seated, Michael got up from his chair and walked around to her. He spoke with a firm and confident voice, "Aunt Beatrice. Would you do me the honor of having a waltz with me?"

There was a look of astonishment, total shock and surprise on everyone's face at the table as well as an audible gasp. You could read it clear as a bell. They couldn't believe he had the audacity to ask her to dance. Every conversation ceased. If the orchestra hadn't been playing, you could have heard a pin drop.

Beatrice saw the expressions then shocked and amazed everyone and extended her hand. "Thank you, Michael. I would like that." She stood up.

The musicians, seeing this, immediately stopped playing and those on the dance floor went to sit down. The room was silent.

As Michael took her hand, he led her to the center of the dance floor. As they stood alone on the dance floor, Michael faced Beatrice, clicked his heels and bowed, turned to the musicians and nodded. "A waltz, please. One not too long." He looked back at Beatrice and gave a huge grin. She looked at him and smiled. A Strauss waltz began and they whirled across the floor.

Everyone watched with mouths wide open in total astonishment.

Jonathan's heart pounded with excitement and pride in the fact Michael took such an initiative. He couldn't have been happier and the expression on his face showed his joy. He could not have been more pleased. It showed Michael had real spunk.

Michael was happy with himself. He had done well in his ballroom dancing classes when he was younger. He whispered a silent, "Thanks, Mom", for making him take the classes. The waltz was over. Michael noted that it was a shortened version of one that is actually about ten minutes long. He stepped back, clicked his heels together, then took Beatrice's hand and kissed it. "Thank you, Ma'am." He gave her a huge smile.

Beatrice smiled and gave a slight curtsy, "Thank you, my dear. That was exhilarating. We must do it again sometime." She stepped close to Michael, took her gloved hands and caressed his face. She pulled his head down slightly, kissing him gently on the lips.

There was a gasp of profound disbelief in the dining room. Everyone was totally speechless.

Michael took her hand and they headed back to the table as the room erupted in a loud applause from the entire company of guests along with their hushed comments.

Jonathan looked right at Michael with pride. He winked his right eye. It immediately became fully clear. He had made the right choice.

To Michael, this last dinner was over much too soon. He had so enjoyed meeting all of Jonathan's friends and especially his aunt. She was definitely a very special lady.

Before Beatrice left the room, she came over to Michael. "It has been a pleasure to meet you, my dear. And thank you so much for the waltz. Until I see you again." She smiled and was gone.

Jonathan handsomely thanked the waiters and musicians and thanked Max profusely again for his excellence, "Max, you are a true treasure. I'm so fortunate to know you and call you friend."

"It's always my pleasure, Mister Jonathan. Glad you approve. I think this celebration was the best ever. May there be many, many more. Be safe on your trip. I'll see you when you return."

"You are absolutely correct. It was the best ever. Thank you for your brilliance."

Max turned to Michael. "Good night, Mister Michael. I am glad you were here." A big smile filled his face.

"Thank you for your kindness. Everything was incredible. Good night to you, too."

They headed back to the pavilion and Jonathan fixed drinks, handing one to Michael. "I must say! You really have won over Aunt Beatrice. I can see she REALLY likes you. I'm SO glad. I think she likes you almost as much as I do. All I can say is, Wow!" He paused for a moment, "You know, I'm going to miss you. I wish I didn't have to go right now but it's very important. Tell me you'll come back again." There was a genuine look of sadness mixed with hope on his face.

"Jonathan. I want to talk with you about something. Something important. Could we sit down for a while?"

They took their seats across from one another.

Jonathan's face expressed concern and worry at the tone of Michael's voice. It was way too serious. He bent his head down afraid he was going to hear disappointment.

Michael began, "I don't know how to tell you how much I have enjoyed the last days. Our horse rides. Our conversations. Meeting your very rich friends." He snickered, "And especially your aunt. She is truly a 'one of a kind'. One for the books. But there's something I've been wanting to tell you. I've been afraid to open my mouth. SHE is the reason I'm sitting here right now and saying what I'm about to say." He paused and sipped his cocktail.

Jonathan heard a calmness in Michael's voice. The fear that roared inside him began to subside. He lifted his head and looked at Michael.

Michael continued, "I have never met a man like you before in my life. I've watched you and talked with you and shared time with you." He paused again and took a big sip of his drink, "And. And I don't want it to end. I know we have only known each other for a very short time and I know I don't have a lot of money. But your aunt said you didn't care about money. But it does bother me. If I am with someone, I want to pull my own weight. I know I don't have the sophistication of those around you but I think I could learn."

Jonathan looked at Michael. His eye sparkled and a big smile covered his face. His heart pounded with joy. Tears filled his eyes and began to run down his face. He bent his head down and cleared his throat a few times, gathering his composure. He took his hand and wiped his face. "Oh, Michael." His deep voice quivered and cracked with emotion. Tears continued to run down his face. "When you started talking, you were so serious. I was so afraid. I... I wasn't sure. Then, you tell me feelings like you are expressing. I'm so happy.

I have searched for someone like you to share my life but thought it was only wishful thinking, just a dream that could never come true. But then, there you were. Aunt Beatrice is so incredible. After I told her all about you. She told me I should go with my heart but I was afraid to act. It's not easy to have the love I want. People just don't understand. I mean, it's not like I want to push it in everyone's face. But she said to say something because you just might say 'yes'." He stood up and looked down at Michael. "Come here."

Michael stood up and moved over to Jonathan. Jonathan grabbed his head with both hands and slowly moved his face to his. Then, he passionately kissed Michael.

Michael wrapped his arms around Jonathan and returned the kiss. When they parted, Michael spoke softly, "I hope no one pinches me. I don't want to wake up." He started to chuckle.

Jonathan wiped his face and snickered, "Now, all we have to do is figure how to work this out. You live down in Atlanta and I live up here. Please, tell me if I sound like I'm pushing or rushing something. But, Michael, life is too damn short. I believe in the concept of striking while the iron is hot."

They sat and talked about the future days ahead and seeing each other on a regular basis. It would help them grow into being together.

"I see we're on the same path. That sounds great." Michael shook his head.

Jonathan walked over to the bar cabinet and grabbed a pencil and some paper then returned to Michael. "Here. Write down your address and I can write to you when I get back from my trip." He handed Michael a small piece of paper. "We can plan for you to come for a visit when... as soon as you can." Jonathan wrote on another piece of paper, folded it up and handed it to Michael along with the pencil. "Put this in your pocket. It's my phone here." He gave a big smile.

Michael wrote his address and phone number on the paper, folded it up and gave it to Jonathan. "Yes. And I can contact you here. I know if I send a letter to the hotel, you'll get it." He placed the pencil down on the near table.

"Maybe you can come with me on the next trip I take. We could go see some of those museums after I finish business. I want to see all those museums with you."

"That would be unbelievable. I would love that. Okay. I know you have to get organized for your trip tomorrow and I should get back to my rooms at the hotel. Hopefully, they haven't given them to someone else."

They headed upstairs and Michael gathered up his things. "I think that's it." He looked around the room.

"If you forgot anything, you can get it the next time you're up here. And I hope it'll be soon." Jonathan's eye glinted with joy.

They went downstairs and went to the door. Jonathan grabbed Michael and kissed him again. "I wish you could see my heart. I've waited so long to find someone. To find you. I've so much to live for now. I was so afraid I'd live and die alone. Now, I have someone to share with. Now, I have you. Today is the first day of the rest of our lives. I'll write to you when I get home from my business trip. Please, see when you can come for another visit."

Michael leaned forward and kissed Jonathan. "Till I see you again. Take care and have a safe trip. And by the way, there was that other place you wanted to show me but we never got around to it." He gave Jonathan a big smile.

"When you come back on your next visit, I'll show it to you then. It's so beautiful and peaceful there. High up on the mountain. Away from everything." Jonathan seemed to look off into space as if being at that special place in his mind. "You must paint it. I know you can do it justice." He pulled Michael close and they hugged and kissed one more time.

"Sounds good to me. Until my next trip up here." Michael turned and started up the path to the hotel. It had to be going on two in the morning. "I sure hope Paul isn't still at the desk?"

Michael did not see Paul when he entered the lobby. "Good. He got some time off." He was rather glad Paul was not there. He so wanted to share all this with him. But he was exhausted. The past few days were quite tiring. He'd see Paul the next day after the weekend guests all checked out.

Entering his rooms, he saw the clock on the dresser. It was just after two in the morning. Shortly, he was lying in bed, reliving the past several days. He was so excited he'd finally met someone, someone who genuinely cared for him and wanted him. This made him very happy. After a moment, he thought about his paintings. Would there be time to finish up the two paintings he'd already started and maybe one more before he left for home on Thursday morning? But all that took a backseat to the joy that filled his heart.

After lying there quietly for a short while, he spoke to the darkness, "Please, don't let this be some dream. Please, let it be real."

He closed his eyes and tried to clear his mind. Finally, he fell asleep.

CHAPTER XIII

When he woke up, Michael looked over at the clock on the dresser. It was after ten. His usual shower, shave and brush teeth routine was slightly altered since he'd left his toothpaste and razor at Jonathan's. He used just his toothbrush. He would buy another tube later that day as well as another razor. Finally, he was dressed and heading downstairs. The lobby was virtually empty. As he walked across the floor, the sound of his boots resounded through the space.

"Mister Michael. How are you? I haven't seen you in a few days. Is everything all right? I was getting concerned."

"Paul, when you can take a break, do I have a story to tell you." Michael's face beamed with happiness.

"Oh, sir. This sounds wonderful. And I can see it on your face. Let me get a few things done here and I'll bring out a pot of coffee for us both. We can sit over there and talk. Martin will take over for me."

Michael sat in the same chair as before near the large fireplace in the lobby. Although the area was in the open, there was a sense of privacy about it. He opened his fleece-lined coat and placed his hat on the coffee table in front of him.

Within fifteen minutes, Paul came over with a large tray, containing a pot of coffee, two cups, cream and sugar, setting it on the coffee table between the chairs. There were several sweet rolls on the tray, too. "I have a feeling you haven't had anything to eat yet. Maybe this will carry you over for a while."

"Thank you, Paul. I really appreciate it. You truly are a very special man."

"Thank you for that, Mister Michael." He gave a big smile.

"By the way, did you get to see the chapel?"

"Yes. I've even started painting it. It's a beautiful building and has the same styling as the hotel but a lot more delicate with all its Gothic ornamentation. I was surprised it was locked."

"It used to be open for years but recently with it being so off the beaten path, it was thought it better to keep it locked."

They both prepared their cups and settled into the chairs. Paul looked excited to hear everything, "Okay, Mister Michael. I have to tell you. You look so happy. Like the cat that swallowed the canary. I just know what you have to say is going to be wonderful. I'm not sure why but I'm glad for you already and I haven't even heard the first word." He paused for a moment then looked at Michael with a questioning expression then spoke again, "I know this may sound strange but there really is something about you. Something different from everyone else. Something I can't put my finger on right at the moment. Somehow, there's a connection but I don't know why. I sensed it the first moment I saw you. But enough of my silliness. Tell me what's happening with you. I want to hear your story."

Michael was trying to choose his words very carefully, not to mention Jonathan's name or that he lived at the pavilion. He basically wanted to cover the highlights of the past days. He began with the first night in the dining room, the horseback riding and the boating, trying to make it sound like his adventure was with another guest at the hotel.

"And Paul. The dinner parties in the dining room were amazing. The music and his guests were wonderful. Wealthy but wonderful.

But most of all, his aunt. She's so regal and just...just...just so elegant. I asked her to dance which blew everyone away. No one knew I had the brass to do it." He chuckled in the recollection, "But what really shocked them was when she accepted and we waltzed. She seemed to float across the floor. Last night was incredible. The party last night was the culmination of the celebration. I forgot to ask what it was all about but they said it took place this time every year and all his friends came to celebrate."

Paul kept watching Michael's face and the joy he projected as he spoke. But a questioning feeling came over him. He didn't speak as he wanted Michael to tell his whole story before he entered the conversation.

"Paul, I gave him the painting of the pavilion. He was so kind and good to me. It was the least I could do. I mean, he spent a fortune entertaining and feeding all his guests. True. He might have been able to afford it but it was nice of him to do it anyway. And he was so proud of the painting. He insisted it be put on an easel during dinner, so everyone could see it. He said he'll hang it in his living room when he gets back from his trip. He had to leave this morning for New York. All his guests left, too. When he gets home, he wants me to come and meet him here for a visit, soon. I can hardly wait. I want to introduce him to you. He's truly a fine person, regardless of how much money he has." He looked at Paul and smiled. His story was over.

"Michael, I think it's wonderful. It sounds like you had a terrific time. And it sounds like a new page has turned in the book of your life. But I have noticed you have avoided using any names." He nodded. "I understand. I'm sure you're trying to keep confidences and I respect you for that. But I do have a few questions." Paul looked down at the floor for a moment then back at Michael. "You say there was a dinner party in the dining room here for the last few nights? A celebration?"

"Yes. A long table was set up each night for all his guests. His aunt sat at one head of the table and he sat at the other. There was music and dancing."

"Was the music provided by the piano?"

"Oh, no. There was the piano and a small orchestra. Great musicians. They must teach them well at the college."

"Interesting." Paul stroked his mustache. "And how late did this party last?"

"Oh, Lord. I guess it went till going on midnight. But Jonathan gave all the waiters a big tip and Max…" Michael stopped, slapping his left hand over his mouth, realizing he'd said names.

Paul dropped his coffee cup and he began to pant hard.

"Paul! Are you all right!?" Michael got up immediately and patted Paul on the back. Seeing he was fine, picked up the broken cup and saucer and placed the pieces on the tray.

Paul took his napkin and wiped up the spilled coffee.

Martin saw the commotion and came over to help. After the cleanup, Martin took the tray away and brought another with napkins, fresh coffee and cups. By this time, Paul had finally recovered.

"I'm fine. I just need to gather my wits." Paul slowly composed himself again.

Michael was apologetic, "Oh, Paul. I didn't mean to tell. It just slipped out. Please. Please, keep this confidential."

Paul looked directly at Michael still with a shocked look on his face. Then, after a moment to compose himself, he softly spoke again, slowly and deliberately, "Did you say, Max and Jonathan?"

"I'm so sorry. I didn't mean to tell. Promise me you'll not tell anyone I said anything. Jonathan. Yes. He lives in the pavilion. He's an incredible man. Kind and caring and considerate. And Max is so wonderful. He's the overseer of the dining room and Jonathan is extremely fond of him. Jonathan said he's the finest chef in the world. But you must know this already since you work here."

Paul cleared his throat a bit before speaking. He looked down at the floor, shaking his head. Then, he looked back at Michael. "Could you describe Max?"

Michael shook his head and his face expressed a look of not understanding why Paul would ask such a question. But he complied and described Max, "Yes. He's about my height, stocky, dark hair, mustache kind of like yours but dark, great smile and in his later thirties. Yeah. He looks like a younger version of you, come to think of it. And, yes. He's married and has a young son who's about five or six years old."

Paul looked at Michael. "Hearing what you're saying is unbelievable but I have another question. Jonathan's aunt. Is her name Beatrice?"

Michael looked questioningly at Paul, "Why, yes. Yes, it is. But you would know this since you work here. I'm sure you've met Jonathan's aunt many times when she would visit."

"And Jonathan is your friend?"

"Yes, but I know you know something about him as you knew the painting I did was of his pavilion. You said his name when I showed it to you. It's one reason I gave it to him. It was a painting of his home."

Paul had a puzzled expression on his face, "Mister Michael. There's something very strange here and I don't understand it. I know you are being truthful. I can see your story is genuine. But there's something very bizarre. I'm lost for words to try and tell you." He paused for a long while. Suddenly, he raised his right hand, pointing up in the air and spoke out, "I remember! I remember! That's why you look so familiar to me! That's why you looked so familiar to me when you first arrived at Sandora. I just couldn't remember. Till now!" His hands trembled. He looked intensely at Michael. "It is you. I now remember." He was silent for another moment, "Mister Michael. I don't know how it happened but you need to know. You need to know the whole story. All of it. I can tell from all you've said there is a true and loving connection between you and Jonathan. But when you know all of it, it will break your heart."

Michael sat totally unknowing, panicking, wondering what Paul could be talking about. What could be so bad? Why was Paul so agitated? Why was he so concerned? What is it he could know that was so overwhelming? "Paul. You have to tell me. What is it?"

"Mister Michael. I will tell you but it's going to sound impossible. I have to think where I should begin, so you'll know it all. Much of it was well known but many who knew have gone. I'm one of the last to know much of the details as it was something told to me often. To tell you and explain it to you, I'm not sure where to begin. But I will try."

"First, you're going to have to clear your mind and take a deep breath. I'm still reeling from what you've said and find it impossible but I know you've told the truth, regardless of how insane it may sound to me. I remember. But hear me out before you say anything.

I don't want to lose track of what I'm going to tell you. You must know it all. I must not leave anything out. It's all too important." He looked right at Michael. "The Max you speak of. Max... was my father."

CHAPTER XIV

"Max was your father!?" Michael's face dropped in astonishment and disbelief. He could hardly speak. He was glad he wasn't holding his coffee or it would've been on the floor. He shook his head from side to side in an effort to settle the information into a stable landing.

Paul continued, "Yes. I remember. And you met the boy, Max's son, in the dining room. You put your cowboy hat on his head. That boy. It was... me. And I remember that hat. It was brown and had a band made up of 'mother of pearl' set in gold links all around it." He looked down at Michael's hat, sitting on the table.

"What?" Michael was speechless for a moment, "But how can that be? How can you know?" He shook his head. The event of just a few days earlier was fresh in his mind. He looked right at Paul, at his hat and the hatband then back at Paul again. He was so stunned at hearing Paul tell of the young boy, meeting Michael in the dining room and saying it happened many years before. He could not speak.

"Yes, it was you those many years ago. It was you who put your hat on my head. And we all laughed. That's why I now know all you have said is true. You were with Mister Jonathan."

Paul fumbled, trying to figure out how to continue and make sense of it all, "To start out, I have to explain. There was no party in the dining room last night or any of the previous nights. And Jonathan's residence has been locked and uninhabited for a very long time."

"I don't understand." Michael's face took on a questioning expression.

"Just wait till I'm finished. Maybe there will be some explanation."

"Okay. I'll be patient." Michael sat back in his chair and listened intensely.

"First, I need to tell you about Jonathan. I realize you know some of it but I need to fill you in on all of it."

"His father was in a loveless and childless marriage but divorce among the elite was absolutely taboo. One day he happened to meet this woman. Yes. And he fell deeply in love with her. Her name was Sandora. She, too, loved him beyond everything else. They kept their liaison secret for many, many years even though she got pregnant early on in their relationship. Jonathan was born as the illegitimate child of an unwed mother and this very wealthy and affluent man. Jonathan was the first-born. A few years later his brother, Paul was born. Both took the name of their mother since they were never told who their father was. Their mother and her lover would have rendezvous while the boys were visiting Beatrice or off at school. So, the boys never saw their father."

"The man was so happy to have sons, he set up lavish trusts for both of them. He always took care of their mother, too. Over half of his wealth went into the trusts and for the care of their mother."

"As the boys grew, they were sent to the finest schools and given the best educations available. They never wanted for anything. They were also taught the meaning of money and its power. Even when they reached an age of understanding, they still were not let in on the secret. There was only one person who knew the whole story. This was the man's sister, Beatrice. She loved her brother more than anyone. She, too, kept the secret but became known to the boys and their mother early on in the boys' lives. She treated the boys like her own sons, watching over them and making sure they never wanted. She allowed the boys to call her aunt but never revealed the connection she had with them and the reality that she really was their aunt."

"Then, there was his eye. When he was away at school, a terrible storm was going through. I think Jonathan was about eighteen then. Some of his friends were watching the storm, standing by a large window. There was a bolt of lightning that hit a tree and it started falling toward the window. Jonathan saw this and reacted. He raced to the window, pushing them out of the way just as the tree crashed through it. His actions saved the other boys but he got hit with branches and broken glass. When they pulled him out from under the branches, they saw the broken glass had cut his eye. The result was the loss of vision in that eye. But this didn't dampen his spirit. They called him a hero but he wouldn't hear of it."

"Jonathan was not allergic to work. Oh, no. He found himself being mentored by a wealthy banker who took him under his wing and helped him follow in his footsteps. Doing exactly what the man said, Jonathan became one of the best financial wizards in the banking industry. He became very wealthy on his own. Many in industry, banking, shipping and railroading came to him for advice and to obtain large loans for their businesses. All of them became rich with Jonathan's help. That's why he had so many affluent and wealthy friends. Beatrice was so proud of Jonathan and his success."

"All was going well until the boys' mother caught pneumonia and died very quickly. It was devastating to both of them."

"When Jonathan was twenty-three, he visited this area and saw how beautiful it was. When he was twenty-seven, he began to build the hotel here in memory of his mother. That's why it is called Sandora. He knew it would be a special place and many would come. It was his way of dealing with his own grief. As you can see, no expense was spared. Only the finest of everything was used. It was finished in two years. The very next year after the hotel was completed, Jonathan had the residence built in the same style. He was thirty years old when it was done. So, you see. The hotel and everything associated with it actually belonged to him."

"As the hotel was being built, Jonathan chose a place high on the mountain that had a spectacular view. It's where he had a chapel built. It was finished the same time the hotel was. He spared no expense in its construction. For example, all the windows were made by Tiffany. They're really quite exceptional."

"To keep his mother near, Jonathan had her moved from the mausoleum where she was originally buried and placed in a stone crypt in the chapel. When his father died, he, too, was moved there. This request was stated in his will and private papers. He wanted to be buried next to Sandora, the love of his life. Even my parents asked Jonathan if they could be laid to rest there. Jonathan would have it no other way. He wanted to have all those there who were loyal and loved. He even prepared a place for himself, so he would be around those he loved in life. So, the chapel ended up being not only a place of quiet reflection but also a resting place for a group of loving and caring people. I'll be the last one placed there as I wanted to be next to my parents. The chapel was so very special to Jonathan. Probably the most special place of all."

"But I have digressed. Let me continue. After his mother's death, Paul went to Europe to try and drown his grief by skiing and drinking but ended up drinking excessively. It was five years later, Jonathan got the message Paul had been killed in an avalanche while skiing. He was only twenty-nine. This was truly devastating to Jonathan.

Everyone realized it was Beatrice who helped him through the pain and suffering. Paul, too, is in the chapel. Jonathan had designed his house with a bedroom for Paul and when Paul died, he had all of Paul's things put in that room when the house was finished."

"Unbeknownst to Jonathan, his father took Paul's trust and placed it in Jonathan's trust. Jonathan, with his trust and his own wealth, became one of the richest men alive."

"Three years later, his father passed. Jonathan was thirty-four. When he died, his will gave much of his money to his legitimate wife but a substantial amount went to Jonathan. His will also declared Jonathan as his son, putting much out in the light and proclaiming how proud he was of Jonathan. Jonathan was glad the man he'd come to know and had been his mentor in business was actually his real father. It all made sense then as to why he'd been so loving and caring toward him. This just allowed Jonathan to glow brighter in the light of his success. It also opened the door for him to realize Beatrice was really and truly his aunt."

"Everyone loved him and everyone close to him didn't care about the fact he was illegitimate. They knew he was a fair man, honest and giving even though he could be ruthless in business decisions. He always sided with the ones he knew were right regardless of their status. He never walked over anyone for his own gains or the gains of others."

"And you're right. Jonathan was a great friend to my father. He met dad a year before the hotel was completed. Dad was twenty-seven and the youngest top chef in Europe when Jonathan happened to eat at the restaurant where he was working at the time. After finishing his meal, he called over the waiter and demanded he meet the chef. Dad appeared, thinking there was some mishap or problem with the food but Jonathan got up, smiled and grabbed dad, giving him a huge bear hug, telling him it was the most incredible food he'd ever eaten. He immediately told him he wanted him to come and oversee his hotel dining room. He wanted him to help with the final design of the kitchen and the layout of the dining room. And he told him he would be paid very, very well."

"Dad was so flabbergasted, he didn't know what to say. And before he could say anything, Jonathan told him to pack up and be at the hotel as soon as possible. He smiled and told him he would see him in a few weeks. He went into his wallet and handed him a huge sum of money, indicating it should cover the expense of relocating then headed out the door."

"And so it was. Mom and dad arrived and he took total control of the entire dining room and kitchen project. Whatever he wanted, Jonathan provided. He always had the finest and freshest foods available. Nothing was out of bounds. The finest wines and liquors. The finest linens, china, silver and other appointments. Everything was the best. And when Jonathan's New York friends came to the hotel and ate, none could believe it. The clientele was immediate. And as word quickly spread of the excellence of the hotel and the dining, everyone who was anyone, from all over the world, came here."

"It was in the fall, a year after Paul's death, Max and his wife had a son. Me. They asked Jonathan if they could, out of respect, name their son, Paul. Jonathan was surprised yet honored. I've tried through my life to be the kind of man Paul was and would've been."

Paul paused for a few moments and shook his head. He poured a new cup and took a sip. "Now, what I'm about to tell you is the issue."

"First, I'll tell you about the celebration you didn't understand. It was a way to share a special time with friends. It celebrated his escape from death. Jonathan always had the celebration, starting on the same date the incident began that almost took his life. He made sure it would last a few days. That's why it started on Wednesday. That was the fourteenth. That date was of extreme significance."

Michael looked at Paul with disbelief and a total lack of understanding. From what Paul had indicated, there had been so much loss for him already, what could have happened that might have made him die?

"Jonathan had been in Europe on business. He had booked passage to return to New York but the business meetings lasted longer than expected and he missed the train back to Paris and then to Cherbourg. This twist of Fate allowed the ship to sail without him. If he had been on board, he would have died."

Michael thought of ships lost at sea on their way to New York but there were only two of significance. "I can only think of two ships going down in the Atlantic. There was the Andrea Doria in July of nineteen fifty-six and the Titanic in April of nineteen twelve." He paused, realizing what he'd just said, "The Titanic was in April. On April fourteenth, it hit the iceberg and sank on the fifteenth." He looked at Paul and realized his age. And if he was the young boy, there could only be one answer. "So, you're telling me Jonathan missed sailing on the Titanic?" Michael's mind whirled with numbers, adding and subtracting to calculate years, "Nineteen twelve. The third celebration. Aunt Beatrice said it was the third celebration. Nineteen fifteen." He looked at Paul strangely. "I can't believe it! I was back in nineteen fifteen?" Michael shook his head. "No wonder everything looked... off. Boating. Damn! I get it now.

That's why he said it was his way of coping. Damn! He was forcing himself on the water, the cold water, to face his demon." Michael was so overwhelmed. All he could do was sit there unable to speak.

Paul spoke quietly, "His aunt gave him a golden Saint Christopher's Medal at the first celebration in hopes to keep him safe in the future. Jonathan even built a small shrine in the chapel dedicated to Saint Christopher. It's quite beautiful."

It slowly became a realization for Michael. He spoke softly, "No wonder everyone's attire seemed dated. No wonder Jonathan had no idea what I was talking about when I asked about a 'clip-on' tie." He shook his head. "They weren't invented yet. You know, it's funny. With all the times I talked with everyone, no one once, not once, ever mentioned a date. We talked about many things but never did a year come up. And I never said one either. I just assumed. Damn! And you know what? Because I'd forgotten to sign and date the painting, no one questioned. Jonathan brought it to my attention when I gave it to him. I told him I could do it another time. If I had, someone probably would've said something and the cat would've been out of the bag. Wow. What can I say?" He looked at Paul. "But how? How did I cross over? Why?"

"Mister Michael, I have no idea how or why. Who knows where Destiny takes us or how the Fates come into play? But now, I have to tell you the worst part. You said Mister Jonathan was leaving for New York to go to a business meeting in Europe. You are correct. He did go to New York and left for Europe on May the first. Come. Follow me. You need to see something."

Michael grabbed his hat. Paul led the way behind the front desk and opened the door to the main office. He pointed to a matted and framed front page of an old newspaper. "This is what I wanted to show you. This is why he's not buried in the chapel. He was never found."

Michael looked and read the headlines. It was as if a thousand daggers pierced his eyes, his body, his heart. He panted, trying to catch his breath.

"Mister Michael! Are you all right?" Paul grabbed Michael's arm to steady him.

"I must go! Somehow, I have to try and stop him!" Michael spoke with conviction, turned and ran out of the office.

Paul called out to him, "But where are you going!?"

He yelled loudly, "If I can, I'm saving yesterday!" He ran through the lobby, out the front door and around the building, heading to the paths that lead to the pavilion.

CHAPTER XV

Michael had to get to Jonathan somehow. What he read on the front page of the newspaper made it perfectly clear. 1915 was the year of the event described. And if he didn't find Jonathan in time, Jonathan was going to die.

Down the paths and steps to the pavilion, he ran. His mind continued to whirl, attempting to fathom and sort all he'd heard and realized. Would the Fates allow him to try and save Jonathan? Would they allow him to go back again to 1915 or had the invisible door closed forever? Had he found everything he'd wanted and searched for in life only to see it fade away just like the headline on that old newspaper, hanging on the wall in the hotel office?

Within minutes, he was at the front door of Jonathan's residence. He reached down and grabbed the latch. Strangely, the door opened. But of course, it would. Jonathan never locked anything. Could this also mean, he was back? He ran in and looked around. There, leaning up against the piano was the painting of the pavilion he'd given Jonathan. He ran over and lightly touched the surface. It was still tacky. "YES!" He yelled out, "Thank you, God!! Thank you, God!!"

He laughed quietly through tears. He was there in the right time. He closed his eyes and tilted his head back. "Oh. Thank you! Please! Help me find him." He raced up the stairs to Jonathan's room. "Damn. I'd never have thought I'd have to do this." He ran to Jonathan's dresser and opened the drawer with the jewelry box. Quickly opening it, he grabbed all the cash and quickly counted it. He opened his wallet and removed the few bills that were there and stuck them in his coat pocket. The bills from Jonathan's box, he stuck in his wallet. He knew the bills dated from his time were not going to fly in 1915. Only money from Jonathan's time would be legal tender.

"Okay, I've got almost eighty-five hundred dollars in cash. I can't imagine needing that much but I want to make sure. Eighty-five hundred was a ton of money back then. But what's the old saying about 'what can happen will happen'? I think I'm ready. No, not yet." He ran into the bathroom, grabbing the toothbrush, the tube of toothpaste and his razor. "Okay. Now, I'm ready." He closed his eyes again. "Jonathan, I promise you. I will pay you back. Every dollar."

He raced down the steps and out the front door. He made sure it was secure before heading to the dining room. Suddenly, he wondered if he would remain in Jonathan's time if Jonathan wasn't with him. Michael had no idea where the door in time was located or what allowed him to pass through it. Running up on the terrace, he opened one of the French doors and entered the empty dining room. Across the room, he saw Max. His heart pounded, knowing nothing had changed. He was still where he wanted to be in time. "MAX!" He yelled, "Max! Help me! Help me!" He ran in his direction as tears streamed from his eyes and he began to sob uncontrollably.

"Mister Michael! Are you all right? What's the matter?" Max grabbed Michael's arm to steady him. "What's the matter? You are a mess."

Michael finally got control of himself and spoke through sighs, "Max, Jonathan left this morning for New York, didn't he?"

Max responded, "Yes. Yes, he did." He seemed confused that

Michael would ask that question, knowing full well that Jonathan was leaving early that morning.

"Oh, Max. Thank you. I wasn't sure it was still Monday." He looked intensely at Max. "I have to get to New York, too. I have to stop him. How do I get there? Please, help me. It's imperative I find Jonathan and stop him. If I don't, he's going to die. I know we could try and call him on the phone but I can't take the chance he might not believe me because the story is so insane. He might completely ignore me and go anyway. That's why I must go in person."

"Mister Michael. Yes. What's happening? Calm down. Catch your breath. Yes, it's Monday. How could you not know that?"

Michael began to settle down. "You wouldn't believe me if I told you." He paused a moment, pulled out his wallet and grabbed a bill of large denomination, holding it up, "Max! Do you have smaller bills I can exchange with you for this? I will need them along the way, I'm sure."

Max went to his cash drawer. "Yes, here are some for you." He handed them to Michael. "Jonathan took the seven-fifteen train this morning with all his guests. It came especially for them. The next one, the normal one, is later tonight around six-thirty. If you don't catch that one, there won't be another for almost a week. Do you want me to drive you down there? It'll only take about twenty minutes."

"Max. I see why Jonathan puts so much faith in you. You know exactly what to do when push comes to shove. You're a true godsend."

Max ran into the kitchen for a moment then reappeared in the dining room. "I had to tell Robert to take over for me while I'm gone. Now. Let's go. It's almost five o'clock now."

"Yes. We must hurry. In case something happens on the way."

During the drive down to the train station, Michael tried to explain to Max the situation, "I know it sounds fantastic and truly unbelievable but trust me. It's real. Somehow, it is real. Now, do you understand why he might not believe me if we talked on the phone?"

Max wasn't sure how to take the story. It made him feel very strange to be sitting next to someone who was telling him he was from the future. He also understood why a phone call would never be adequate. He did know something was afoot and if he could help prevent Jonathan's death, regardless of how crazy it sounded, he was willing to go through hell for it. "You know, I could drive you to New York but I don't think the truck here would make it. It's not in great shape and has been through a lot so far."

"Max, trust me. I'll pay you back one of these days. And not a problem. I don't think it would make it, either. I just hope it gets us down to the train station. But thanks for the offer." Michael was incredibly anxious, "This burden is mine and mine alone. But I would appreciate it if you'd do one thing for me."

"Anything, Mister Michael. What?"

"Wish me lots of luck that I make it."

"I will, sir." There was a silence for a few moments before Max spoke up again, "Mister Michael. I don't want to seem to pry into things, not my business. But I must tell you. There's something special about you. I mean, for Mister Jonathan. I've never seen him so happy as when he's with you. Never before has he been so joyful and excited about life. I'm so glad and happy for him. He truly deserves happiness and to know and feel that someone cares deeply for him. I believe you are the one. If anyone can save him, you can. I truly believe the Fates have sent you from the future, somehow, to do just that and to be with him."

"Oh, Max. What a wonderful and kind thing to say. You truly are his friend. If I can accomplish this mission and stay here, I hope one day I'll be as good a friend to you as he is to you."

Finally, they arrived without incident. Michael got out and leaned into the truck, grabbing Max's shoulder. "Thank you again. Thank you ever so much. I owe you." He paused slightly then looked directly at Max, "And, Max. You have an incredible son. HE is the one who understood. If it were not for your son, I would never have known and this would not be happening right now. And most likely, Jonathan would die, for sure. It is Paul who has set these wheels in motion. I hope I can repay him one day, too. You take care. Bless you, for being such a good friend to Jonathan." He turned and ran into the building.

Max didn't completely comprehend what Michael had just said. As he pulled away on his return to the hotel, he pondered all he'd heard.

Michael stopped short, having to catch his breath. His heart was still pounding and he was shaking like a leaf. He composed himself before walking over to the ticket window. "One ticket to New York, please." He got out his wallet and paid the fare with the largest denomination the man would take, so he could get smaller bills in change. He put the bills in his wallet and the coins in his pants pocket. "Thank you so very much."

"Will there be any luggage, sir?"

"Oh. No. Thank you for asking, though." Taking the ticket, he went over and sat on a nearby bench. He placed his hat next to him. After a few minutes of fidgeting, he got up and went to the window again. "Excuse me, sir. Will there be an announcement for the train?"

"Yes, sir. Don't worry. We won't let you miss it." The gentleman smiled.

"Thank you. Thank you very much." Michael smiled back.

There was a large clock on the far wall. Michael watched the hands. They seemed frozen in place. But after a while, he realized they really were moving. Slowly. But they were moving.

He was so agitated he couldn't sit still. "Maybe if I walk around some." He put his hat back on, got up and walked out onto the platform. Up and down a few times, then back inside and he sat down again. "I'll bet I look really strange getting on a train to New York with no luggage and dressed like 'Midnight Cowboy'. Oh, well."

Time seemed to crawl but eventually, he heard the sound of the train approaching the station. His stress level started back up again. He hurried out onto the platform as the announcement was made, regarding the arrival of the train. A puzzled look came to his face as the engine approached. There on the front of the engine was a panel with three large numbers in white. "Four-o-seven. Interesting."

Finally, he boarded and started down the aisle of the passenger car. There was a conductor coming his way. Michael smiled, "Hello and good evening."

"Good evening, sir. And where are you headed this evening?"

"New York." Michael held up his ticket.

"Please, head up three cars. That car will go all the way. It'll save you time in moving later. Some of these other cars will be transferred to other trains when we get to Richmond as they have other final destinations."

"Thank you. Thank you so much for your help. But one

question. Do you have something soft? I was going to take a nap and I don't have anything to put my head on. It's been one of those days."

"Certainly, sir." He gave an understanding nod. "I understand how those days can be. I'll bring you a little pillow in a few minutes."

"Again. Thank you so very much." Michael watched as the conductor headed down the aisle. He then walked to the appropriate car. When he got there, he looked around. It was only half full, so he chose a seat and moved in against the window.

Shortly, the conductor reappeared and handed Michael a pillow. "Have a pleasant rest, sir. There's time for a very long rest. I'll wake you if it's necessary."

"Thank you, again." Michael took the pillow and positioned it between his head and the window and closed his eyes. After a while, he could feel the lurch of the train and they were off.

CHAPTER XVI

Michael had no idea what time it was when he awoke to the severe shuddering of the passenger car and the train, coming to a screeching stop. The jarring almost knocked him out of his seat. "What was that?" He muttered, "Whatever it was, it's definitely not right." It was still dark outside. He didn't see anyone running frantically through the train. "Guess there's no mass murderer on the loose." He snickered to himself, repositioned his head on the pillow and closed his eyes again.

After a few minutes, he heard someone walking down the aisle. It was the same conductor. "Excuse me, sir? Are you awake?"

"Why, yes. Actually, I just did wake up. I know something's wrong. What was that huge vibration and screeching noise?"

"We're just south of Richmond. It seems there is some problem with the engine. Someone is checking on it. I heard a comment it has somehow derailed. We should know shortly."

Michael sat quietly for some time until the conductor reappeared.

"It seems there's something severely wrong. The engine did derail. A good thing we were not traveling faster or the whole train could've gone off the tracks. Could've been a disaster. It's a mess, though, as it is. We can't go on. Someone has left to walk up to find help and see what can be done. I'm pretty sure we'll be here for some time. You might as well try to get some more rest."

Several hours passed before the conductor came by to wake Michael. "Sir, there are several wagons and coaches outside to take everyone to the Main Street Station in Richmond. Proper authorities have been notified. For those of you, heading to New York, they're sending another train south to pick everyone up. But I hear it won't be for a few days. There's going to be a lot of rerouting since this train is now blocking the main north-south line. I'm so sorry for the inconvenience. This is such a rare event."

This information was extremely unsettling to Michael but he tried to stay relaxed. Somehow he would get to Jonathan. He knew this was pushing the envelope somewhat but he did have time and wanted to think positively. He spoke calmly, "Thank you so much for the information. You've been extremely helpful. When I get to the station, I can make reservations at one of Richmond's hotels. I used to be rather familiar with the city. It should be interesting to see it now."

❦

It was early Tuesday afternoon by the time Michael reached Main Street Station. He was told another train wouldn't arrive there until Thursday night and would leave around eight-thirty. They had him listed to be on board. That would be April 22nd. It was the same day he was supposed to leave Sandora and head back to Atlanta. He shook his head. It just dawned on him that the 22nd of April in 1982 was the same day in 1915. "I wonder if that is significant? How many other years did all the days in April fall on the same date?"

After a pause, he took stock of the moment and realized The Jefferson Hotel was right up between West Main and West Franklin but it was too far to walk. There was time to take a trolley. What a treat it would be. And The Jefferson Hotel was one of the premier hotels in Richmond. He remembered people talking about how elegant it was when his parents lived in Richmond, during his college years at Virginia Tech. He also remembered someone once telling him the main staircase of the hotel was used in the movie, 'Gone With The Wind', but he wasn't sure how true that was.

By late afternoon, he was walking into the hotel. He paused for a few moments and looked around. "I have to admit. It really lives up to the terms elegant and spectacular." And there it was in the main lobby. The staircase. "Definitely! It sure does look like the one in the movie." He walked over to the reception desk.

"May I help you, sir?" A young man stood behind the desk. He looked Michael up and down in his cowboy attire.

"I sure hope so. I was on the way to New York and the train was waylaid. So, I have to spend a few nights here in Richmond. I would gratefully appreciate it if you had a room for tonight and tomorrow night."

"Certainly, sir. Yes, we do. It's the middle of the week and a room is no problem. So, you were on the train that derailed south of town?"

"Yes. It happened sometime during the night, I think. I mean, it was still dark." He shook his head. "I'm so sorry that I sound so crazy but things are rather stressful for me right now."

"I'm glad you're all right, sir. Please, sign the register and I'll get you the key. You're alone?"

"Terrific! Yes. It's just me. Let me pay you in advance." He pulled out his wallet. "Would it be possible to get small bills back? I will need them in the future for tips and such."

The young man responded, "Not a problem."

Michael continued, "I do apologize for my appearance. These are the only clothes I have right now. Is there any way I can have them cleaned and pressed? I'd like to know if there's a place I might purchase more." He paused for a second then realized, "Oh, I forgot. Miller and Rhodes is on East Broad Street, isn't it?"

"Why, yes sir. It is. We can take care of your clothes with no problem. One of the staff can accompany you to the store if you like."

"That would be wonderful. If my clothes can be ready by morning, I'll go down to Miller and Rhodes tomorrow. Thank you." Michael signed the register. "If someone could come up with me, I can give him my clothes."

"Not a problem. Thank you, Mister Groves. You're in room four-o-seven." He hit the bell on the top of the desk and a young man came immediately. "Eric will go with you." He looked at Eric. "Eric, this is Mister Groves. He will be staying in room four-o-seven." He handed him the key.

Michael found it rather interesting. Four-o-seven was his room number at Sandora.

Eric was a dark-haired young man with a dark mustache. He was around nineteen, with bright brown eyes and an infectious great smile. He was as tall as Michael. "Good day, Mister Groves. Hope you had a pleasant trip." He looked all around on the floor. "Mister Groves. Where are your bags?"

The man behind the desk spoke up, "Mister Groves doesn't have any at present. Show Mister Groves to his room, get his clothes and take them to be cleaned and pressed."

As they got on the elevator, Michael looked at Eric. "Eric. Please, call me Michael. Mister Groves just sounds too stuffy and you look like a pretty hip and cool guy."

Eric looked strangely at Michael. "Hip, cool?" He shook his head. "But I'm not cold."

"Oh. I'm sorry, Eric. 'Hip' means you're on top of things. You're aware, in touch with everything, fun, interesting. 'Cool' means you're great, all right, fun to be with. We use these words where I come from. Yeah. Totally 'groovy'. Oh. That basically has the same meaning."

Eric chuckled, "Sounds like you're a pretty… hip and cool guy, too, Mister Michael." A huge smile filled his face, "Groovy."

They both were laughing as they left the elevator and headed down the hall. Being with Eric transported him back to his college days when he was nineteen and the conversations and words he used back then. He realized the reason he'd never used them around Jonathan and his friends is because they use a language that is not… loose. Yes. That's a good way of putting it. Loose.

Michael and Eric entered the room. Michael went immediately to the bathroom and turned on the faucets to the tub. He took the razor, toothbrush and paste out of his jacket pocket along with the paper currency and placed them on the sink counter. Removing his clothes, he wrapped a towel around himself. Gathering his clothes, he went back out into the main room and handed them to Eric. He took his wallet that was sitting on top of the clothes and pulled three one-dollar bills out of his wallet and gave them to Eric.

Eric looked at the money and very loudly spoke out, "Thank you, sir! Thank you very much, Mister Michael!" He bowed slightly. He skirted by Michael and ran into the bathroom, grabbing Michael's boots. "I'll fix these right up for you, too, Mister Michael. And if you need anything else, please, let me know." He headed for the door.

"Eric, I have to go to Miller and Rhodes tomorrow morning. Would it be possible for you to accompany me there? It has been many years since I've been to Richmond. I know it's down on East Broad Street but I don't remember how far it is."

"I'd be happy to, sir."

"I'm exhausted and I'm going to bed shortly. How about you come up tomorrow around nine and bring me my clothes and we'll go from there. I'll call down to the front desk and tell them the plan. Would that be cool?"

"Certainly, sir." He paused a moment and he gave a big grin, "COOL! Yes, Mister Michael. That would be... COOL! I will see you tomorrow morning at nine. Have a good rest, sir. Goodnight, sir." Eric turned, looking at the light streaming through the window then back at Michael and spoke in a questioning voice, "Good day, sir?" He smiled.

Michael laughed, "Thank you, Eric. See you later, alligator. Till tomorrow morning." He gave a 'thumbs-up'. "Cool!"

Eric gave a questioning look, regarding what he just heard but then laughed and gave a 'thumbs-up', "Cool! Groovy!"

Michael joined in the laughter as Eric left the room.

Michael closed the door, walked over to the desk, placed his wallet on it, got on the phone, called the front desk and told the gentleman of the plan. The next day was supposed to be Eric's day off but there would be no problem. They would have Eric work the next day and give him another day off.

He went into the bathroom. The tub was already half full of very warm water. As he lay in the water, he began to reflect on all that had happened and his quest. He whispered softly, "Jonathan, I cannot let anything happen to you. You really are the one I've searched for all my life." He paused with everything racing in his head, "But who would have ever thought I'd find you some thirty-one years before I was born." He shook his head in disbelief.

The water was cooling by the time he got out and dried himself. He took the razor and ran it over his neck under his chin. He tilted his head up as he looked in the mirror. "Yep. That'll do."

He went and crawled in bed. In no time at all, he was asleep.

CHAPTER XVII

There came the sound of a knock at the door, waking Michael. He could not believe he'd slept right through the night. "Just a minute." He quickly went to the bathroom for a towel to wrap around himself before going to the door.

It was Eric, carrying his clothes and boots. "Mister Michael, I polished your boots real good, too." He paused for a moment, "Mister Michael, I didn't see any undergarments. I hope they didn't lose them." He spoke with apology in his voice, "Oh, and here's some coins you had in your pants pocket. I heard it make noise as I was turning them in. I saved it for you." He extended his hand toward Michael.

They were the coins he got back in change when he bought his train ticket on Monday. Michael just smiled, "Why don't you just keep them." He was extremely pleased with how honest Eric was and gave a 'thumbs-up' with his right hand. "I'll also explain about the no undergarments."

"Why, thank you, sir." He stuffed the coins in his pocket. "Might I ask what that was you did with your right hand?" He mimicked the gesture. "You did it yesterday and I was going to ask you but I knew you were tired."

"It's a hand gesture we use to let people know we are really pleased about something. It's like 'hip' and 'cool' and 'groovy' with your hand."

Erick laughed, "I love it! That's so cool!"

They both laughed as they both did a 'thumbs-up'.

Michael continued, "Now, about my undergarments. No. They did not lose my underclothes. The fact of the matter is, I rarely wear them. When I was in school, at university, my roommate didn't wear them. He told me they made him feel uncomfortable. So, I tried it. And you know what? He was right. Especially, at night, in bed. We call it, going 'commando'." Michael chuckled, recalling those days at college in his mind.

"Really?" Eric's face was filled with surprise, "You know, I think I'll try it. 'Commando.' That sounds pretty hip and cool, too. Groovy."

They both began to laugh.

"Thank you so much for making my boots look great. I do appreciate it. Just a second. Let me get dressed." Michael continued to talk as he took his clean clothes and went into the bathroom to brush his teeth and put on his clothes. He also stuck the paper currency back in his jacket pocket. "Eric, why didn't you tell me before you left yesterday that today was your day off? It's very thoughtful of you to come and help me when you could be home and not working. I'm actually glad management asked you to work today. With your help, I know it is going to be a terrific day." Shortly, he came out, fully dressed and sat on the edge of the bed to put on his boots.

"You were kind to me, Mister Michael. And I hope you don't mind me saying it but I think you're a really hip and cool man." A big smile was on his face, "I have to tell you, too. No one has given me such a handsome tip before. Something tells me it will be a fun day. I don't mind doing it at all. It's my way to say thank you for being kind to me."

Michael finally got his boots on and they were out the door and headed down to the lobby. Michael stopped by the front desk to thank them for letting Eric work on his normal day off, so he could go with him. He also found out basically where Miller & Rhodes was located. Eric already knew the way. Then, it was off to the store.

Although it was two blocks north and about six or seven blocks east, Michael thought they would walk. The day was nice and they had plenty of time. It also gave Michael the chance to see a bit of Richmond in this time period.

On the way, they passed a shop and Michael could smell coffee. "Eric, we're going in here first." It was a little restaurant. They were seated at a small table and Michael ordered coffee and sweet rolls for them both.

"Why, thank you, Mister Michael."

"You're more than welcome. I had to eat something, as I didn't get to eat at all yesterday." He thought for a moment, "Actually, I haven't had anything to eat since Monday morning. And I have to have my coffee. Seems I can't function without it."

"Mister Michael. I'm sure they would have brought food to your room if you liked."

"Yes, I'm sure but I wasn't that hungry. I'm really not that hungry now. But I know I have to eat something. I think it's because I have so much going on in my head." He took a sip of coffee and ate part of a sweet roll. "So. Eric. How long have you been working at The Jefferson?"

"I started about a year ago. I finished school and wanted to save some money, so I could go to university. I would like to be an architect one day. I did very well in school and everyone said I should go to university. My mom and dad are very proud of me but were sorry they couldn't afford to send me."

Michael responded, "Interesting. I studied architectural

engineering when I was in college… university. If you have a creative mind, you will definitely enjoy it."

"Yes, but it's so expensive. One day I will go. I just need to save up enough money." He gave a reluctant smile.

"I was lucky. My parents paid for my entire education. Not many are so fortunate. But don't give up your dreams. You just never know what might happen down the road."

"What about you, Mister Michael, if you don't mind me asking? I find it so unusual for a man like you to be traveling without baggage. And you seem very occupied with something."

"I am on a very strange quest. Very strange. It might sound rather cliché but it truly is a matter of life and death. If I told you the story, you would think I was crazy and probably be afraid to be with me. I'm the one on the quest and even I find it difficult to believe it. What can I say?"

"Well, I have a feeling you will do what you must and complete your quest. You strike me as a man who doesn't give up."

"Thank you. Wish me luck. I truly am going to need a lot of it." He sipped more coffee then looked at Eric and started to snicker.

Eric looked at Michael. "What? What's funny?"

"Here. Lean forward. You have some of the sugar icing stuck in your mustache from one of the sweet rolls." Michael took his napkin and wiped Eric's mustache.

"Oh. Thank you, Mister Michael. Yeah, I know it's the curse of having one. And it drives me crazy when coffee gets sucked up into it, too. I have to take my tongue and try and suck it out." He shook his head and began to giggle.

"Keep your mustache. It's a small price to pay for having one.

You look very handsome with it. Now, what gets me is when I eat ice cream. What a mess that can be."

"And that's the truth!" Eric started laughing out loud.

Soon, they finished their coffee and rolls and were off again.

Michael was amazed when he walked into the store. It sure was different from the Miller & Rhodes he remembered from the 1960s, the last time he was in the store. He smiled, shaking his head.

"Is something funny, Mister Michael?"

"Yes, it is. But it's part of the strange quest I mentioned."

A very nice gentleman directed them to men's clothes. Michael started looking through them and finally found two pairs of pants and two shirts. Then, he got a few pairs of socks. "I guess I need a satchel to carry them in, don't I? And I need some shaving soap, too. I already have my razor."

The gentleman, helping him with the clothes, directed him to the place he could purchase a small suitcase then indicated where he could get the toiletries.

The shopping done, Michael put everything in the small suitcase and they headed back to the hotel. Eric insisted on carrying it. Michael dismissed Eric at the front desk but not until he handed him fifteen, one-dollar bills. "Thank you, Eric, for being so helpful today. I could not have done it without you. I'm so glad The Jefferson has wonderful employees such as you. And don't worry. You are ambitious. You will have that money to go off to university soon enough. Mark my words. Don't you dare give up your dreams." He spoke loud enough, so everyone behind the front desk and within earshot could hear his appreciation. Michael was quite sure one of them was the manager on duty. Again, it was his belief that praise should be given when it was well deserved.

"Thank YOU, Mister Michael. Thank you so very much." He bowed. "And remember. If you ever need anything in the future, please, let me know." He smiled and gave a 'thumbs-up'. "You're so hip and cool, Mister Michael. Groovy!"

"Eric, I will. I will make sure you are the first one I call for. You never know. I may need a good architect one of these days down the road." He smiled at Eric and gave a 'thumbs-up'. "Eric. Hip and cool. So are you. So are you. Not to worry. I can take the suitcase with me to my room. Goodbye, Eric, and thank you."

Eric called out, "Goodbye, Mister Michael, and thank you so very much. Good luck on your quest." He paused for a moment, grinned, pointed at Michael and said, "See you later, alligator!"

Michael, too, gave a big grin, pointed at Eric and responded, "After 'while, crocodile!"

They both gave a 'thumbs up' and just roared with laughter.

Michael finally turned and headed to his room.

Michael stayed very low-key that night, calling down for something light to eat as he knew he didn't have the proper attire to eat in the elegant dining room.

The next morning, he arose and dressed in his regular clothes. He would save his new ones for another time and left them in the new suitcase along with the razor, toothbrush and paste. On with his boots, hat and coat, he was out the door to catch his train. He stopped at the front desk to check out. They had given Eric the day off since he'd worked his regular day off to help Michael. Michael called over the manager, "I want to thank you so much for accommodating me the last two nights. And thank you so much for having such terrific people like Eric on your staff. He is definitely a plus for your establishment."

"Thank you, Mister Groves. It was our pleasure. We do value excellence in our staff. I'm glad you approve of Eric. He is truly a hard-working young man."

Michael continued, "Eric very much desires to go to university to study and improve himself. I hope you will consider keeping him as an employee during the summer months before he returns to university in the fall."

"I have no doubt there will be a place for him here as long as he wants to work here. Thank you for speaking for him. That is very kind of you. Please let us know if you ever need any accommodations with us in the future." He smiled and gave a slight bow of his head.

"I surely will." Michael smiled and slightly bowed his head.

It was going to be another long wait since the train was not going to leave until eight-thirty that night. He checked in at the ticket counter. Michael sat there waiting but thinking of what he was going to do once he got to New York. Murphy's Law kept intruding his thoughts. Yes, there was that fear of his plans not going smoothly. Regardless, he would face whatever obstacle got in his way.

It was late morning on Friday when the train pulled into Penn Station. It had made several stops and layovers due to the previous accident, changing the normal runs and car transfers.

Leaving the station, he walked up to the corner of Thirty-Third Street and Seventh Avenue. He knew he had to get to the Waldorf Astoria at Thirty-Fourth Street and Fifth Avenue. It was only a few blocks away. Jonathan's aunt had a suite of rooms there. Jonathan had mentioned this during one of their conversations while at his pavilion. She always insisted on him staying with her while he was in New York.

He did realize his attire did not look like the kind one would be wearing to enter such a prominent hotel and ask questions. But he was determined to find Beatrice and Jonathan. He knew they would want to know what this was all about. So, up one block and over two and he'd be there.

Finally, standing in front of the building, he looked up at the façade of the structure. "It's funny to think. This is where the Empire State Building is going to be erected in a few years. What can I say?" He nodded before entering the front doors.

As he walked over to the front desk, he saw the concierge look him up and down. He spoke quietly, "This is not going to be pretty, I'm sure." Finally, he stood at the front desk, placed his suitcase on the floor then cleared his throat before speaking, "Excuse me, my good man. I would like to leave a message for Lady Beatrice Stanenberg. It is extremely important and of the utmost urgency. Please, excuse my attire but my travel has not been kind. I would also like to have a room if at all possible. I would also like to pay in advance."

There was a questioning expression on the young man's face, "Yes, sir. We do have a room available."

"Oh! Excellent! I am so glad. Thank you."

"Would you please sign the register? And how many nights would you like to be here?"

"My job must be completed by next Saturday morning, the first.

If it isn't, either way, I will be gone. So, let's see. That's eight nights. Yes. Eight nights."

Michael signed the register, pulled out his wallet and opened it, exposing the large amount of money there. The expression on the young man's face changed drastically when he saw the large amount of cash. Michael knew that money spoke silent volumes.

The young man cleared his throat, "Sir. I am so sorry." He shook his head. "I was not sure." He looked Michael up and down again.

"I totally understand, young man. But seriously, my trip has not been what I expected. The train derailed and wrecked in Richmond. It's a long story."

"I'm glad you made it through with no injuries." The young man then changed the subject, "How is it you know Lady Stanenberg? I have seen many of her friends but I have never seen you before."

"I know her through her nephew, Jonathan Wolfe."

"You know Mister Jonathan? Oh, sir. I didn't know."

"Yes. I need to see both of them as soon as possible. It is most severely urgent. And I know this may sound crazy but it truly is a matter of life and death."

The young man looked down at the register. "Mister Groves. Lady Stanenberg is out and will not return until next Friday and Mister Jonathan has gone upstate. I don't think he will be returning until he gets back from Europe. I have no way of reaching either of them right now. But she will be back Friday evening. I will let her know immediately when she arrives."

"Thank you. Ah."

"Oh. Sorry, sir. My name is Gerald."

"Thank you, Gerald, for being so helpful and understanding. I truly appreciate it. I must tell you I do not have the proper attire for the dining room. Is there some kind of alternative?"

Gerald smiled, leaned forward on the desk, looked around to see if anyone was listening then spoke softly, "When you are ready to eat something really good and tasty, come see me. I'll direct you to a place where the food is not fancy, not expensive but it's quite exceptional."

Michael leaned forward at the desk and spoke quietly, "Thank you, Gerald. Thank you very much." He handed Gerald four single dollar bills.

"Thank you. Thank you so much, Mister Groves. You are so very welcome. I can tell you are a really nice man. It seems that those who know Lady Stanenberg are most generous and kind. If you need anything, anything at all just ring down and ask for me. I can have a bellboy show you your room if you like."

"Thank you, Gerald, but that won't be necessary. As you see, I travel light." He looked down at the small suitcase on the floor. "And please. Call me Michael."

Gerald handed the key to Michael. "Yes, Mister Michael. That will be room four-o-seven."

Michael looked at the key then back at Gerald.

Gerald saw the odd expression on Michael's face. "Is there something wrong?"

"Oh. No. It's just... nothing. Nothing at all. Thank you." Michael grabbed the suitcase and headed to the elevators. As the elevator opened, he stepped in and looked down at the key again. "Room four-o-seven. Humm. Four-o-seven. Same as at Sandora and The Jefferson Hotel. Same as the train. Could there be some connection?" Was it part of the puzzle or just some strange coincidence? He thought for a moment. "Damn. Maybe there is something to it. This whole adventure started when I got to Sandora. On April seventh. Yeah, the fourth month and the seventh day. Four-o-seven. And what are the chances that nineteen eighty-two had the same days and dates as nineteen fifteen? Damn. Maybe they have been the Fates giving me signposts, leading me to Jonathan all along, showing me I'm on the right track. God only knows."

Michael took the elevator to his floor and was soon in his room. Placing the suitcase down near the desk, he wondered where Jonathan was and why he'd gone upstate. "I know he's here on business. But, damn. Why upstate? I guess I'll have to think about that tomorrow." He paused for a moment before speaking, "'Afta all. Tamarra IS anotha day!'" Michael shook his head and laughed out loud.

CHAPTER XVIII

For the next few days, Michael went out into the streets to get a feel for the time. Old cars, trolleys and the clothes were something to see. His cowboy hat and boots did draw attention but he wore it anyway. He was living in history. Even the newspaper headlines about the war in Europe and if the United States would get involved brought memories of pages from the history books. He even took a trip over to see the Statue of Liberty. A stop at one of the banks allowed him to change several of the larger bills into a large amount of one-dollar bills to use for tips.

The place Gerald recommended to eat was excellent. Michael could not believe the prices of food in 1915 as compared to his own time. But he then had to remember, pay for average workers was not in the five figures or higher like in 1982.

He was stuck between a rock and a hard place. He had no way to contact Jonathan and with Beatrice out of town, he was at a standstill.

Finally, it was Friday afternoon, April 30th. He sat in his room, pondering when Beatrice would return. Panic was beginning to set in. Had he come all this way only to lose the prize? Could the Fates be so cruel to bring him to the banquet table only to deny him all the wonderful foods there? It was the eleventh hour and something had to be done.

He called down to the front desk. It was Gerald. "Gerald, how are you today? I just wanted to find out what time it was and if Lady Beatrice had come back yet."

"It is twenty minutes after four. I am sorry, Mister Michael. She hasn't shown up yet. But I definitely will tell her the minute she arrives. And I will tell her it is extremely urgent."

"Thank, you, Gerald. I do appreciate it. Thank you."

Without removing his clothes, Michael lay on the bed. His mind whirled as to what he was going to do. Would it work? Could he change the past? Could he save Jonathan? And if he could, how would it affect history? His eyes closed, trying to calm himself but his anxiety was driving him crazy.

After a while, a loud knock was on his door. Michael was startled. He sat up quickly. He heard the knock again.

He quickly went to the door and opened it. There stood Aunt Beatrice. Seeing her questioning expression, suddenly, all the mounting stress let go and Michael began to crumble. He started to shake, tears rolled down his face and he started crying uncontrollably.

She looked at Michael with distress, "Michael! What is wrong!? Gerald called me over when he saw me arrive and said there was a guest here who had an urgent message regarding Jonathan. I couldn't imagine who it would be. Then, he said it was a man who wears a cowboy hat and boots and his name is Michael. I knew it had to be you. What is wrong and so urgent? And look at you! You're a mess!"

He couldn't stop shaking and crying but spoke through tears, "Aunt Beatrice. I'm so afraid. I don't want to lose him. We must stop him. He cannot go. He cannot go." His hands were fumbling with one another and he spoke through his sobs, "I can't lose him. I can't let him die."

Beatrice realized Michael was totally distraught and immediately grabbed his arm. "Michael!!! Tell me!! What is wrong!? Get hold of yourself! What is the matter? What has happened?" She led him into his room and sat him down on the bed. "Tell me what is wrong!"

"Aunt Beatrice. He's going to die. Jonathan is going to die if I don't find him." He continued to sob.

"Michael. Take a deep breath. Just calm down."

Michael began to gather his wits and began to breathe regularly. He wiped the tears from his face and eyes.

"That's good. Now. Come with me. We're going upstairs. I think you need a drink." Beatrice brought him to the elevator and up to her apartment. Entering her living room, she led him to a chair. "Here. Sit down. I'll go fix you something." She picked up the phone and called down to have a tray of food brought up. They could also bring up her luggage from the car.

She handed him a glass of cognac and sat down, looking right at him. "Now. What is going on?"

"Aunt Beatrice. I must find Jonathan and stop him. If he leaves tomorrow, he is going to die. I must find him. I know you must know where he is."

"He's up in the Adirondacks, gathering important papers and will not be back in the city until tomorrow morning. He'll be going directly on his trip. He and Alfred have a big business venture and they have to finalize everything overseas before anything gets worse in Europe. But what is going on? How did you know how to find me? I truly don't understand. What's going to happen? How do you know? Please. And what do you mean when you say Jonathan is going to die?"

Michael began to try and explain. "One time while Jonathan and I were talking, he mentioned that you lived here. That's how I knew." But before he could get into his story, there was a knock at the door. It was one of the service personnel with a rolling cart, containing trays of snack foods and fruit. Two more, each with a trunk on his shoulder, were behind the one with the food cart. Beatrice directed them to take the trunks into her bedroom. When finished, she thanked them all and gave them a gratuity before leaving.

Over the next few hours, Michael took all the pieces of the puzzle and put them together for Beatrice. The final piece was the old newspaper story, hanging in the office at the hotel. He also explained how he knew it was true. He knew the history. "I know how insane and impossible all this sounds but know I tell you the truth."

Beatrice's face turned ashen. She realized however ridiculous and unbelievable it all sounded, Michael was being straightforward about it all. She sat silent, shaking her head.

"Aunt Beatrice, for some reason, the Fates have allowed me to find Jonathan and come to know him. And, yes. If I dare say it, to fall in love with him. I mean, this is all impossible. I can't believe this strange quirk would happen for no reason. I can't give up. I had no idea my feelings for him were this great until I saw the newspaper and knew if I didn't act, I would lose him. Forever. I couldn't let that happen."

"You stay here tonight and you can go early in the morning and find him. Departure is not supposed to be until ten. I'll have someone drive you, so you'll have no problem getting there." She went to the phone and made a call to her driver. He would be there to pick Michael up in the morning.

She looked lovingly at Michael. "I knew you were special. I knew you'd be good for my Jonathan. I just didn't realize how special you really were. Would you like to rest some before you go?"

"Oh. No. I'm so wound up right now, I couldn't sleep on a cloud. If you don't mind, I'd just like to sit here and wait till early morning then go. And by the way, with research I've done, I already know it will not leave at ten. There will be a delay and it will not leave till noon."

Beatrice looked at him strangely. "You know that?"

"Yes, it's weird to sit here and know the whole future. What's sad is I doubted I'd be able to change it in any significant manner. Even when you tell people a possible outcome, they never listen. No one wants to believe the worst can actually happen, especially to them. It always happens to someone else. Not them. And if you make some major gesture to prevent an event, they think you're some crackpot, wack job and lock you up."

Beatrice spoke quietly, "I had planned to rest after my trip but all of this has me completely agitated. There is no way I would be able to shut my eyes, knowing Jonathan is in danger. I am too overwhelmed to sleep. I'm going to sit with you. We can talk some more. I'll call down and have some coffee and more food sent up. A big pot."

They sat, ate and drank coffee all night long, talking.

Beatrice told more about Jonathan. She was so happy he finally came to know who she really was. With his accomplishments, she became more and more proud of him. She also told of the conversations she'd had with him, regarding Michael.

Michael was so grateful to hear it. It just reinforced the knowledge that Jonathan truly cared for him and loved him.

Finally, the night was over and it was time to take action. Beatrice turned to Michael. "I have been thinking about it all night long and I'm going with you? I know where we can park and I will wait. I would love to go with you to find Jonathan but speed is of the essence and you will be able to move more quickly than me."

"Yes. Oh, yes. That would be wonderful. I know you will have an influence there I could never begin to match. Thank you. I love you for it. With your help, we will save Jonathan."

"I think we will." She smiled.

Suddenly, the phone rang. It was the front desk to let Beatrice know her car had arrived. They gathered up what they needed and headed down. On the way, Michael stopped by his room and got his coat and hat.

Within fifteen minutes, they were at the front of the hotel. The car was waiting at the front entrance.

Michael stood in awe, "Geez! Aunt Beatrice? This is your automobile? It's beautiful. What is it?"

"It's a Packard. The four forty-eight. It's a really nice car. I got it last year. They didn't make many of them as they were a bit pricey."

It was early morning, May the 1st, and the car headed south. "Thomas, Pier Fifty-Four, please." Beatrice instructed her driver.

"Yes, Ma'am."

When they pulled up, Beatrice saw an official she recognized. He saw the driver and came over to the car. "Oh, Lady Stanenberg. Are you heading out this morning?"

"No, not me. But my nephew, Jonathan, is. It's extremely important I find him before he leaves. Would it be possible for his friend, here, to go search for him?"

"That would be fine. If you'd like, you can wait right over there until he does. Your driver can park there." He pointed to a spot. "Yes, I saw Mister Jonathan earlier this morning as he was boarding. Oh, by the way. Departure will be at noon. There has been a slight delay because of some transfer."

Beatrice looked at Michael. "It seems you are absolutely correct. This is rather scary. Chills just went through me."

The driver drove into the place indicated by the official and turned off the motor. Michael got out. He took her hand and kissed it. "It might take some time but we'll be back as soon as I find him."

"Godspeed, my boy. Godspeed. It's just after eight but don't tarry. It's a big ship and a lot of places to look."

"Sir, let me take you to the boarding ramp." The official guided Michael to the right place. "Go up and you should see someone who can help you from there. Make sure you listen to the call when they tell everyone to leave or you'll be stuck there."

"Got it. Thank you ever so much, my good man. You will never know just how helpful you have been." He quickly handed the man several dollars.

"Why, thank you, sir. That is very gracious of you." He bowed his head slightly. "Seems all of Lady Stanenberg and Mister Jonathan's friends are kind and generous people."

Michael was off and up the ramp when he saw a young man with a large pad in his hands. "Excuse me, sir. I'm trying to find Mister Jonathan Wolfe. Is there any way you can help me? It's extremely urgent."

The young man looked down at the pad. "Mister Wolfe is always in first class. Here, you may be able to find him in his suite." He pointed at a room number. "If he's not there, try the veranda café up on the boat deck. He always likes to have his coffee in the mornings. You have some time as we are slightly delayed. We will not be leaving until noon."

"Thank you so very much. You're right. He's most likely in the café. That's where I'll go first. He likes his coffee in the morning. What is the best way to the café?"

The young man explained how he could get there.

"Thank you. Thank you again for your help." He handed the young man a few bills.

The young man smiled, "Thank you so very much, sir."

Michael wound his way and was finally at the café's entrance. Walking in, he looked all around frantically. "Where can he be?" He spoke out loud.

There was a man sitting alone at one of the small tables who saw Michael and how agitated he was. He looked to be a similar age as

Jonathan. "Sir, is there someone you are looking for?" He raised his hand, motioning for Michael to come to his table.

"Oh, thank you. Yes, I'm looking for Jonathan Wolfe. It's extremely urgent. I know he usually has his coffee in the morning. He's someone who can't do without it."

"Oh, you're so right there." The man chuckled, "Jonathan just can't seem to function without his morning coffee. But he just left to go back to his room."

"Oh! Damn!" Michael slammed his right fist into his left palm.

"Don't worry. I was just finishing my coffee and was heading back myself. His room is right down from mine. If you want to wait here, I'll tell him you're here waiting for him. Who are you?"

"Oh, yes. There is time. I'll wait here. I'm sorry. Michael. Michael Groves. He may seem surprised but tell him it's the cowboy." He waved his hat in the air. "He will know you're not kidding him that way."

The gentleman got up, smiled and looked Michael up and down, "The cowboy. I swear. Jonathan never ceases to amaze me." He turned and left the café. Michael sat down at the table.

Immediately, a young waiter came over. "May I get you some coffee, sir?" He removed the used china and silverware from the table.

"Oh, yes. Please. There will be two of us." He smiled at the young man.

"Very good, sir." He bowed slightly and left the table.

Michael began to tap the table with his fingers in an agitated, rhythmic, strumming fashion, starting with his little finger and ending with his index. Moments seemed to last forever. He grabbed the table and tried to pull it closer to himself. It wouldn't move. He looked at the table and couldn't imagine why he couldn't move such a small table. Then, he realized. Many of the pieces of furniture on ships are bolted to the floor to prevent them from moving in rough seas.

He was a nervous wreck. After a while, panic grew. Was he smart to wait? Just sitting? Was he wasting precious time? He kept looking at the doorway. He began to take deep breaths, sighing loudly. His heart began to pound faster and faster.

The waiter returned with a tray with a pot of coffee, cups, sugar and creamer, napkins and silverware. He poured a cup. "Will there be anything else, sir?"

"No. No. Thank you so much."

The waiter bowed again and walked away.

Suddenly, Jonathan was standing in the doorway, looking around the room.

Michael saw him come in and quickly stood up. Just as Jonathan turned in his direction, Michael ran up to him. "Jonathan!" He stopped short, resisting the desire to grab him and hug him tightly. Tears began to run down his face. He spoke softly as he was sobbing, "Jonathan. Oh, Jonathan. I was so afraid. I was so afraid I might not find you." He paused for a moment then spoke in an even softer voice, "Jonathan. I love you! I love you more than anything, more than words can express. I didn't know how much until I knew I might lose you. You cannot go. You cannot go. You cannot leave." Michael's body was shaking like a leaf and he was panting hard.

Jonathan grabbed Michael's upper arms with both hands and looked directly into his eyes. He, too, spoke softly, "Michael. It's you! And you love me? You truly love me?" He paused for a moment and smiled, "But how? What is wrong? Why are you so upset? You're a mess. Why are you here? How did you get here? What is going on? I thought you were headed back to Atlanta?" He released Michael from his grip. "I thought Alfred was joking when he said you were here but when he said it was the cowboy and you waved a brown cowboy hat in the air, I knew it was true. Here. Sit down. Talk to me."

They both took a seat at the table. Michael began to calm down and catch his breath.

Jonathan poured a cup and looked right at Michael. He shook his head. "Now, tell me. Something is obviously not right. I don't understand. What's going on? And why are you so upset and agitated?" He took a sip of coffee then looked right at Michael again and smiled, "And you love me? You love me. Wow!"

Michael looked into Jonathan's eyes and spoke softly but firmly, "Jonathan. Yes. I love you. It's the reason I have come all this way. To stop you. We have to go. Trust me. I know if you stay here, you're going to die! And they'll never find you."

Jonathan's face expressed shock, "What!? What are you talking about? Now. Slowly. Calmly. Tell me what you're talking about. Die? How am I going to die?"

"Jonathan, it is May the first. I saw the old newspaper. The newspaper hanging in the main office at Sandora. Paul showed it to me. But, of course, you have no idea what I'm talking about. It hadn't been hung yet when you were there. But it was the newspaper. That's when it all became clear. I knew. Only then did I realize that THIS is the same year. It is nineteen fifteen."

"Well, of course, it's nineteen fifteen. What year did you think it was?"

"I'll get to that soon enough. I know you're not going to believe it as I still find it difficult to believe myself. If it weren't happening to me, I would think it was insane. What I'm getting at is this. You must get off this ship. Now! This ship is going to leave here today. And on May seventh, it is going to sink. And you are going to drown."

Jonathan looked right at Michael. "Drown? Sink? What do you mean, sink? How is it going to sink? Don't tell me it's another iceberg. Yes, wouldn't that be ironic!" He gave a quick shake of his head. "But what are you talking about?"

"Just off the coast of England, it will be hit by a torpedo from a German submarine. It will sink in less than twenty minutes, taking over a thousand people with it. And, you're supposed to be one of them."

Jonathan looked questioningly at Michael. He still didn't seem convinced. "What? That's crazy. Don't be ridiculous. Yes, there are problems between Germany and the rest of Europe but there's nothing happening between Germany and the United States. And they'd never sink a passenger ship loaded with Americans. That is unheard of. It's uncivilized."

"I tell you. It is one big reason the United States enters the war. The sinking of this ship is the tipping point. You and I are sitting right here... on the Lusitania."

"This is insane. How could you know this? Do you have some crystal ball? You never told me you were psychic." He had a questioning expression on his face. But looking back at Michael, he could see Michael was not kidding. He was dead serious.

"I have something better than a crystal ball. I have history. Jonathan, I tell you now. You must get off this ship. I'm here because I..." He stopped and looked around to see who might be listening.

There was no one. "Because I love you. YOU are the one I have looked for all my life. I know that life without you would be one without real happiness. If you don't come with me, I will stay here. I will die with you. I cannot imagine my life without you."

Jonathan could see the truth and sincerity on Michael's face. "But, I don't understand. How do you know for a fact this ship will sink?"

"You asked what year I thought it was. Well, I know all this because I'm not from nineteen fifteen. I'm from the future. As crazy as it sounds, I'm from nineteen eighty-two. And I have proof." He reached into his pocket and pulled out his wallet, setting it on the table. "Okay. Look inside."

Jonathan was shocked at the comment, "The future? Nineteen eighty-two? Are you delirious? You have to be kidding me. Michael. Are you ill?" He looked hard at Michael. He looked down at the wallet and opened it. He took out several bills and looked at them. "Well, I see these bills are current. So?"

"Oh, sorry. Those are yours. I had to go into your dresser. I knew my money wouldn't be good here and I needed money to travel and pay for things. I promise I'll pay every dollar back to you. Here." He reached into his coat pocket, pulled out the few bills he had there from his own time and put them on the table. "And when you finish looking at them, check out the rest of my wallet."

Jonathan picked up one of the bills, looked at it carefully and saw the date. His eyebrows showed his questioning. He looked right at Michael. Then, he opened the wallet again. He pulled out a plastic card. Examining it, he turned back to Michael. "What is a Mastercard? And what is it made of?"

Michael laughed nervously, "If not used carefully, it's something that gets many folks in serious trouble with bill collectors." He paused for a moment, "It's a credit card. Plastic money. The card is made of plastic. That's why we call it plastic money."

"Credit card? Plastic money?"

"Yes, we use them in place of money. A long story. I'll tell you later. Please, Jonathan. We must go."

"Not until I understand more."

"Okay. Look at the credit card. You will see two dates stamped on it. One is the date it will expire and the other shows when I became a cardholder."

Jonathan spoke softly, "You have been a member of this card since… nineteen seventy-five. And it will expire in… June, nineteen eighty-four." He put the card on the table and looked hard at Michael.

"Keep looking." Michael insisted.

Jonathan went back to the wallet. He pulled out Michael's driver's license. "The picture is in color. Looks like they took color photography to a much higher level. Yes, the picture is you. Georgia driver's license. For what? And it's made of the same plastic."

"Black and white and sepia photos are virtually a thing of the past. Everything is in color now. And the driver's license, we have to get one to allow us to drive a car. If you don't have one, you can be arrested. Another long story. I'll tell you sometime."

A look of total surprise came to his face, "It indicates you were born in nineteen forty-six. That's thirty-one years from now." He looked back at Michael. "If it's nineteen eighty-two for you then you're thirty-six. Two years younger than me."

"Jonathan. We don't have time to joke around. Do you think I could fake all this? And for what reason would I do it? You must get off this ship. You must come with me. Your aunt is waiting down there. Waiting for us both. She believes me. That's why she drove me here to help me find you. I don't think you realize how much she truly loves you."

"You really are from nineteen eighty-two? Tell me about it. Aunt Beatrice believes you? How did you find her?"

"JONATHAN!!! We must get off this ship!!!" He shouted. Suddenly, he realized how loud he was and looked around to see who was looking at them. No one else was in the room. "Just trust me. You told me where she lived in one of our conversations. Now, come with me. We must leave."

Jonathan shook his head. "Wow! This is unbelievable. Who could have ever imagined? It is obvious you are telling me the truth and I get it. We really do need to leave the ship. But if it's going to be hit with a torpedo, we must try to stop it from sailing."

"It will do no good. They HAVE been warned. The German Embassy posted a bulletin in the newspaper, warning everyone and still, it will set sail. By the way, who was the gentleman who came to get you? I must thank him. I might never have found you without his help. We must warn him."

"That's Alfred. He and I are… were… going on a business trip together. It's very important with what's happening in Europe. He was going alone but thought we'd have more influence if we both showed up. Come, let's run to his room. We still have time. They have not made the call to go ashore yet." He called the young waiter over, "Young man. Leave the ship. Save yourself. It is going to sink." He handed him several dollars.

"Thank you, sir." The young man looked at them very strangely as they ran out of the room and headed to the first-class suites.

Jonathan pounded on the door. "Alfred! Alfred!" He kept pounding.

Shortly, the door opened. "Jonathan? What is the problem? I see you found your friend."

"Alfred, we have to get off the ship. Trust me. Come with us. Please. We must leave."

"Jonathan, don't be ridiculous. We have to go to the meeting. You know how important it is and everything is on board for the meeting. The ball is rolling on this. We cannot stop it now. If one of us is not there it will…"

Jonathan interrupted, "Alfred! If you are dead, it won't matter what happens at the meeting."

"What do you mean? Dead?"

"The ship is going to sink. The Germans."

"Yes. Yes, it's been in the papers. It's all propaganda. No one believes it. They would never sink a passenger ship. It's absolutely uncivilized."

"But Michael knows it's going to sink."

Alfred looked at Michael. "Well, how does he know?"

Jonathan didn't think. He just blurted out, "He's from the future."

Alfred immediately got a bizarre look on his face. "Jonathan. I think you need to go have a drink. Please. I have things to do before we sail. I'll talk with you later at dinner." He shut the door in their faces.

Jonathan pounded on the door again. "Alfred! Alfred!"

Alfred's voice came through the closed door, "Go have a drink. Don't be ridiculous. I'm not coming. I'll wire you from London on the progress of the meeting. This has to be done and it cannot wait. You know that."

Suddenly, there was a young man coming down the hallway announcing for everyone not sailing to go ashore.

Jonathan looked intensely at Michael. He turned and pounded on the door again. "Alfred! Alfred! Alfred Vanderbilt! Come with us!"

"Go away. I'm not coming. Everything is underway and I'll be fine." The door opened and Alfred looked sternly at Jonathan, "You know how important this is. I must go, regardless. They're waiting and counting on us. You do not have to be there. You were only coming for moral support. I MUST be there. They know who I am and they are expecting me. If I leave the ship now and the package gets to London without me, no one will know what to do. There will not be enough time to take another ship and keep the plan in motion. I will be careful. If something does happen, I'll get to safety. Don't worry."

Jonathan grabbed Alfred and hugged him, "I understand. Just be safe, my friend."

"Thank you, Jonathan." He closed the door.

Michael spoke, "Jonathan, there's nothing you can do. You tried."

"I know. But he's right. He has to be there with the package."

They quickly moved through the hall and finally to the boarding ramp. Down they went and shortly, they were at the car.

"I was so worried." Beatrice called out, "Come. Get in. Let's go home."

Jonathan turned and looked in the direction of the ship. "Alfred. Good luck, my friend. Take care and be safe." He shook his head and got in.

As the car headed to the hotel, everyone was quiet until Michael spoke softly, "I wonder what this is going to do?" He looked down at the floor of the car.

"What?" Jonathan looked at Michael with questioning on his face.

"I have done it." Michael continued to speak softly, "Yes, I did. History has been changed. I wonder how it will affect the future?" He looked right at Jonathan then Beatrice. "I hope it's for the good. Maybe now, it will get there and not sink. Maybe the war will not happen."

All were silent in contemplation the rest of the trip back to the hotel.

Finally, they were back in Beatrice's apartment where the conversation resumed, "I've been thinking." Jonathan spoke up, "You're right. About what has been done to the future, to history but we will never know. Only those who live in the future will possibly know of any changes. And hopefully, it will not matter. Maybe they will never realize there's a difference."

"I will know. If there is a significant change, I will know. I will know what it should have been." Michael cringed. Then, he thought of Alfred. "Jonathan. I'm so sorry. He who hesitates is lost."

"Sorry?"

"About Alfred. He was one of the most highly publicized passengers when the Lusitania went down. What was so important he wouldn't come with us?"

"It was something dealing with a secret financial matter. It involved millions and had to be done immediately because of the coming conflict. Alfred was involved and knew it would be beneficial if I got involved. Everyone thinks he's going over for financial reasons but that was a cover for the real reason. Now, I guess it doesn't matter. That issue is now moot. But maybe he'll make it."

"Jonathan, I really am sorry. I can't give you false hope." Michael paused for a moment then spoke again, "I know it may sound weird but I have always had this attraction to the sinking of the Titanic and the Lusitania. I have read so much about both of them. I even have a model of the Titanic. I know many who are Titanic buffs." He saw the questioning on the faces of Jonathan and Beatrice. "I'm sorry. 'Buffs' refers to a bunch of people interested in the same thing."

"Michael, that sounds absolutely ghastly. I can't imagine why people would be interested in such matters. It sounds morbid." Beatrice announced her disapproval.

"I know. But people are people. I can't tell you why or what makes them tick. Do you know that in my time, there are people looking for the Titanic? Back in the early nineteen-fifties, there was a movie called 'Titanic', starring Barbara Stanwyck and Clifton Webb. Another one in the late nineteen-fifties was based on the book by Walter Lord. And two years ago there was a big movie called 'Raise the Titanic'. It was a kind of spy story where they had to bring up the Titanic from the ocean floor. I loved it. The effects were great."

Jonathan cut in. "You have to be kidding? Movies?"

"Yes. Moving pictures. They have come a long way by nineteen eighty-two. A far cry from what exists right now in nineteen fifteen. I'll tell you more about them sometime."

"This all seems so unreal. Are you absolutely sure? I know you showed me all the stuff in your wallet but it still seems unbelievable. Impossible. Insane."

"Jonathan?" Michael looked right at Jonathan. "Do you believe what I said to you on the ship?" He peered directly into Jonathan's face.

"Yes. Yes, I do. That's why I know you wouldn't lie to me. Especially, about something like this."

"I understand. But wait until Friday. Then, you will know." There was a short period of silence then Michael spoke softly again, "And instead of drowning at sea and never being found and after a long life, you can be buried at Sandora in the chapel like you planned." He gave a big smile to Jonathan.

Jonathan took on a look of reverie, "You know that place is very special to me. It's the place I wanted to take you but didn't get the chance before I left. It's the place I wanted you to paint."

"Strangely enough, Paul told me about it and I have almost finished the painting. It was the painting number three I told you about but never got into details as to the subject matter. Actually, it's going to be a really nice canvas when it's done." He paused for a moment, then spoke out again, "Damn! It's back there! In nineteen eighty-two. Or should I say 'up' in nineteen eighty-two? I'll have to start over and paint it again."

Beatrice and Jonathan looked at Michael with smiles on their faces.

Jonathan looked at Michael. "Who is Paul?"

"He's the concierge at Sandora. Max's son."

Jonathan shook his head and his face filled with question, "Max's son? But he…" He began a mental calculation, "Ah, yes. I get it. He must be in his early seventies."

"I'd say that's about right. And he's a wonderful man. A spitting image of Max. Just older. Maybe that's why I didn't make the connection when I first met Max. Paul speaks very highly of you.

He helped me understand what had happened and made me realize if I didn't take action, you would die. He is the one who showed me the newspaper, hanging on the wall in the office. If he hadn't done that, I'd have never known you were traveling on the Lusitania. I'd have gone home to Atlanta and lost you forever."

"It's funny. Paul remembered that we had met in the dining room and that I had put my hat on his head. It had already happened. But now that I have actually changed history from this point on, it'll most likely be different in the future."

"You see, I had no idea you were in nineteen fifteen. No one ever mentioned a date. A year. I just assumed everyone was in nineteen eighty-two since the dates and days were the same as nineteen fifteen. And you had no idea I was not from nineteen fifteen because we never said anything that zeroed in on the year. I did wonder about your telephone but thought it was just in keeping with the decor of your house or that maybe you just liked old-timey things. It was of no major importance to address it. It's the same for the phone here in Aunt Beatrice's apartment. Because I'd forgotten to sign and date the painting I gave you, we never knew. I had no idea the celebration was because you had missed the Titanic. I didn't find that out until I talked with Paul. But it was the front page of the newspaper in the hotel office that clinched it all together and I knew I had to do something."

Michael paused for a moment then continued in a quiet voice, "I just happened to think of something. I wonder if my interest and research in the Titanic and Lusitania had any influence in me being the one to come to nineteen fifteen to save Jonathan? Is it possible the Fates stepped in for this to happen?"

"You could be right." Beatrice spoke softly, "The Fates truly have played a significant role in all of this. And Michael is the instrument in which everything has been possible to change the events. It seems impossible. But here it is. There's much to ponder."

CHAPTER XIX

Beatrice had Michael move into her apartment to share a room with Jonathan. She always had a room set aside for Jonathan, so he had a place to stay when he was in New York.

The spacious apartment was appointed with period French furnishings of the Louis XV and Louis XVI styles, highly ornamented ceilings as well as paneled and ornamented walls. There was a wonderful grand piano, too. Beatrice said she had it so Jonathan could play when he stayed with her.

Over the next few days, Michael told of the future. One thing they could not imagine was how Michael thought Jonathan was heading to Europe. He was thinking Jonathan was going to fly out of New York. He had to explain about jet airlines and that it took only about six hours to get to London. He even drew pictures for them, so they could see what a Seven-Forty-Seven jet looked like. They were flabbergasted when he told them that it could hold several hundred people. It was a long way from the Wright Brothers at Kitty Hawk just eleven and a half years earlier. Telling of the landing on the moon, really made them sit in awe. Future history kept them on the edge of their seats through the weekend and all the next week.

Jonathan indicated by knowing what was to come, they could make unbelievable amounts of money with the proper investing. Michael agreed and understood why Jonathan would be thinking in those terms. After all, he was a financier.

Jonathan began thinking about the future with Michael. His

face would light up, talking about all the things they would do together.

Michael, too, was excited. He knew he had found the person he wanted to spend the rest of his life with even if it meant he probably had to stay in the past. This proved to be the case when they eventually returned to Sandora and found the invisible door in time was no longer there. Something told Michael the Fates wanted him here in 1915 and the past is where he would remain for the rest of his life. That being the case, he knew he was going to have to be careful. His secret couldn't be known. Only Beatrice and Jonathan could know. There was no telling what would happen if that kind of news got out. This truth was also extended to Max with whom Michael had already pulled into confidence on the trip to the train station. Max always had Jonathan's back.

⸺⸺᭡᭡᭡⸺⸺

It was Tuesday and they were sitting having coffee in the living room when Michael broke the conversation, "Aunt Beatrice, I've noticed the artworks you have from the first day I visited. Jonathan said you had a nice collection. Do you mind if I look at them? I didn't want to seem presumptuous. But the portraits…" He pointed across the room. "That one. Those brush strokes. I know this is going to sound ridiculous but I'd swear it was painted by Vincent Van Gogh. And that one." He pointed at another one. "It looks like a Renoir."

"Michael, of course. Please, go right ahead." She smiled, "And you might be surprised."

Michael got up and went to look at the paintings up close. He looked closely at the five portraits of a beautiful young woman with striking features, raven black hair and intense green eyes. It reminded him of the beauty of Elizabeth Taylor. "These really are incredible."

"Believe it or not, they are of me." Beatrice gave a shy chuckle.

Michael looked closer at the paintings and saw the signatures of the artists. He gave a loud gasp and turned to Beatrice and Jonathan still sipping their coffee, "These signatures! You have to be kidding! They can't be real!" A stunned look was on his face.

Jonathan smiled as he spoke up, "Trust me. They are."

Michael looked at each portrait, moving to each one, calling out the name of the artist, "This one IS a Renoir! A Monet! Van Gogh! Gauguin! Cézanne! You're kidding!?" He looked around the walls at the other paintings and could see many of them done by the same artists. "And those, too?"

Jonathan shook his head in the affirmative. "Yes."

"So, you like my little collection?" Beatrice got up from the settee and walked over to Michael.

"Holy cow! They must have cost a fortune. I mean, paintings by these artists are worth millions in my time period."

"Why, what do you mean? They were given to me."

"Given to you? Oh. That's right! Jonathan said the ones you have were gifts." Michael was amazed. "Wow! Geez!"

"When I was much younger, many years ago, I was in Paris and met Renoir. We had a great time. Pierre-Auguste is a wonderful man. We would meet at a certain café and talk for hours. He knew the others and over a few years introduced me to all of them. I think it was during that time I grew a great fondness for artists with furry faces." She smiled then reached over and caressed Michael's beard with her left hand.

She walked over and sat down on the settee. "I still correspond with them, now and then. Except for three. Paul Cézanne passed away in nineteen-o-six and Paul Gauguin in nineteen-o-three. And poor Vincent. It's so tragic. He was so lost in his own world, so tortured and troubled. He cut off his ear because he was in love with Gauguin and he knew Gauguin was not in love with him. I'll have to tell you about him one day. You know, everyone thinks he shot himself. But we knew differently. He had invited me down for several days. We had a wonderful conversation. He came to where I was staying to have dinner the night before he got shot. He was happy and in good spirits. So, when it happened, I rushed to be with him and talked with him just before he died. His brother, Theo, came when he heard the news to be by his side. It was an accident. A horrible, tragic accident. He wanted people to think it was self-inflicted. It kept a young boy from being punished for mistakenly shooting him. It was an accident. Vincent truly was a gentle soul."

Michael was virtually speechless. "You knew them? I think that's so amazing. Meeting and knowing some of the most famous painters of this time in history. Geez. As to Vincent, I guess Don McLean will have to rewrite his song since Vincent didn't commit suicide. Yeah."

Jonathan and Beatrice looked strangely at Michael.

"I'll explain about that sometime." Michael shook his head.

"Well, Michael. I hope to have at least one of yours hanging here before too long. At least one." Beatrice waved her right hand in the direction of the walls.

"You're kidding!! My painting! Hanging alongside Monets and Renoirs! WOW!! What can I say? I promise you. You'll have more than one if you like."

"Yes, I would like that." She paused for a moment, "And maybe we can all go for a visit, so you could meet Pierre-Auguste and Claude sometime."

"Geez. You know, I keep forgetting they're still alive. That would be incredible." He sat down in a chair near Jonathan's.

"And one day I'll have to tell you some of the adventures I had with all of them." A twinkle came to her eyes and a sly smile to her face.

Jonathan flexed his eyebrows a few times. "Yes, Aunt Beatrice was no wallflower in her younger days. She was quite the adventuress."

It was now quite clear the comment she'd made that day in the dining room at Sandora. It was the one about 'loving artists with furry faces' running in the family.

They both looked at Beatrice. She just sat there with the smile still on her face and a slight blush.

They all began to laugh.

Beatrice smiled at Jonathan, changing the subject, "Jonathan, play something for me. You haven't touched the piano in ages."

"Yes, I'd love to hear something, too." Michael began to clap.

"Okay. What do you want to hear?" He looked at Beatrice.

"My dear, anything you want. Whatever it is, I will love it."

Jonathan sat down at the piano and played a superbly perfect *Fantaisie Impromptu* by Chopin. With the last notes fading in the air, the room was silent. Then, Beatrice and Michael applauded and cheered loudly.

Jonathan turned on the bench and looked at Michael. "Now, it's your turn."

"Michael plays?" Beatrice looked over at Michael with surprise then back to Jonathan. "You didn't tell me he played the piano."

Michael blushed, "Well, compared to Jonathan, it's rather anticlimactic. What can I say?"

"Michael, play something for me." Jonathan got up and smiled at Michael.

"Yes, Michael. Please. I'd love to hear you play." Beatrice was excited.

"Well, all right. If you insist." Michael took Jonathan's place at the piano. After a moment, he began.

The strains of *La Vie En Rose* sounded from the instrument. On the repeat, in his fairly decent tenor voice, Michael sang it in French. On the second repeat, he sang it in English. One last repeat was played again with just the piano. Then, Michael sat silent.

"Michael, that was wonderful. And I didn't realize you could sing and your playing is beautiful." Beatrice spoke her approval.

"Thanks for the kudos but it's obvious Jonathan can play rings around me all day long. I do believe learning and playing gives a greater appreciation for those who are truly gifted and exceptional." He gestured his hand in a gracious manner toward Jonathan. "My piano teacher would've loved to have had you as a student. You could be a concert pianist if you put your mind to it. Hell, you're one already." He gave a big grin.

Jonathan looked at Beatrice. "I didn't know he could sing, either. Surprised me!" Jonathan's face expressed how proud he was of Michael, "I didn't recognize that song. *La Vie En Rose* was it?"

"Yes. It was made very popular by Edith Piaf."

Beatrice looked over at Jonathan then back at Michael. "Who is Edith Piaf?"

Michael began to chuckle but shortly he was laughing out loud, "I'm sorry. I'm sorry. I didn't even realize what I've done." He shook his head and began to calm down. "*La Vie En Rose* was a very popular song in the late thirties and early forties. That's the nineteen-thirties and forties. Edith Piaf is the one most associated with it." He paused a moment then chuckled again, "It hasn't been written yet."

Jonathan and Beatrice had surprised expressions on their faces.

Jonathan spoke with humor in his voice, "But of course, it hasn't been written yet. Why didn't I already know that?" He rolled his eyes, realizing Michael's knowledge of the future. "And what of Edith Piaf?"

"Oh. She was born in nineteen fifteen." Michael paused with a big grin on his face, "Yep. This year. Edith Piaf was born... this year. She had a rather tragic life. I'll tell you about it one day."

"Michael, that was great. Play another." Jonathan smiled.

"Yes, please." Beatrice joined in the request, "Play something else that hasn't been written yet." She began to chuckle and looked at Jonathan.

Jonathan nodded. "Just think of all the music we can hear that hasn't been written yet."

"Okay. Okay. I'll play one more. I'm going to play a song that came to my mind the very first time I saw Jonathan across the dining room at Sandora. It will always be special to me." He looked at Jonathan. "Do you know? When I saw you sitting there, smiling at me, I actually whispered the start of the song." A big grin filled his face, "The song is *Some Enchanted Evening* from the Rogers and Hammerstein musical called 'South Pacific'." He paused for a moment, "And it will not be written until late in the nineteen-forties."

Michael turned and played the introduction before starting to sing the lyrics, changing every 'her' to 'him', "'Some enchanted evening... you will see a stranger... You will see a stranger... across a crowded room.'" He did his best to play and sing well, expressing the full meaning of the song as he would periodically look over at Jonathan. With the last series of rolled chords, moving up the keyboard and building to a crescendo, he sang the last line, holding the last word the full count of the note, "'Never let him… go.'" He ended with the last six big bravura chords in a slight retard, sounding the title of the song. As the music faded, he looked over at Jonathan and smiled.

Jonathan's face was filled with joy and a tear ran down his face. He spoke softly, "I hope you never let me go." He walked over as Michael stood up from the piano and gave him a big hug, kissing him passionately. He whispered, "I do love you. More than words can say."

"What a beautiful song. I understand how you feel. Such a wonderful way to tell someone how special they are to you." Beatrice applauded. "I truly look forward to hearing more songs from the future."

Michael commented, "I must tell you that the song in the play is sung by a guy regarding a woman. As you see, I took some liberties and changed it a bit." After a slight pause, he added, "Just remember, we have to keep it a secret."

"Well, I sure could use a good drink." Jonathan went to the phone and called down for room service. He returned and sat down. "I ordered cracked ice and a pitcher of cocktails for each of us." A big grin came to his face.

Beatrice and Michael looked at each other and clapped loudly as they all cheered.

Finally, Friday came. The news started arriving as a whisper. Like something unsure. But the headlines on Saturday, May 8th, of the New York Times, told the story. Beatrice called down to the front desk for someone to run out and get a copy for her.

There was a knock at the door and the bellboy handed her the paper. "Here is your paper, Lady Stanenberg. You will see. It is terrible." He bowed politely.

"Thank you so much, Albert." She handed him a gratuity.

"Thank you, Lady Stanenberg! Thank you so much!" He bowed quickly, turned and skipped down the hall.

Beatrice brought in the paper and displayed the front page to Jonathan and Michael. "My dear. It looks like you were absolutely correct. Just like you said. What can I say?" They all peered at the picture of the liner, covering a large portion of the page and read the bold headlines where Alfred's last name was very prominent.

"Maybe I haven't changed history that much." Michael had a questioning look on his face. He turned to Jonathan. "I know I have asked you this before. What was so important that Alfred wouldn't come with us? He didn't even want to listen to us. You said it was some financial thing but something tells me that there is more to it than that."

Jonathan shook his head. "I guess it doesn't matter now. Nothing can stop it."

"Stop it?" Beatrice looked right at Jonathan.

"We had a plan. A plan to stop the coming conflict. But now, nothing can stop it." Jonathan shook his head. "Even you didn't know. I had to keep it secret. No one could know. It was too dangerous."

"Okay. You have your aunt and me totally in left field. What was it all about?"

"Not many knew about Alfred's and my meeting upstate. And those who did thought it was about paperwork for a financial deal in Europe. Even those close to Alfred didn't know what it was actually about. All they knew is he had a very important meeting that had to be kept secret. It's why he wasn't at the celebration at Sandora. He was up there, getting everything organized. We were meeting with regard to something that could possibly have changed the entire course of the coming war. He and I thought it might even stop it in its tracks. We were meeting to finalize the plans."

"You are kidding!" Michael was shocked, "What the hell could've been so fantastic? Does it have to do with the 'package' Alfred was talking about?"

Jonathan got up and poured more coffee for everyone then sat down. "Yes. But let me start at the beginning. It really started over two years ago. Everyone in the financial and industrial world knew there was terrible unrest in Europe. Then, last June with the assassination of Archduke Ferdinand of Austria, we knew a major war was coming and how devastating it would be to all the economies of the world. But no one knew what to do. That's when Alfred came to me, regarding a scientist in his employ. The guy had an idea for an incredible device that most certainly could have a significant impact. Alfred knew that with the money we had together, we could sponsor the development of this thing and develop it quickly. Alfred said he'd do the footwork and get it going."

"The device the guy had invented was strictly theoretical as there was no way to test it without major complications. If it actually worked, Alfred realized how significant it could be in slowing if not halting any conflict. With the direction of his scientist, Alfred assembled very secret groups. I have no idea how many groups there were but each was separate, not knowing the existence of the others. And they were located in different areas of the country. Each group would produce a specific part, never knowing exactly what they were making. Only Alfred and his scientist had the overall picture and knew how the parts would go together. When each part was completed, it would be packed, shipped to New York and kept in a location known only to Alfred. After all the parts were gathered together in New York, they would be sent to England. Alfred and the scientist would accompany the shipment. A secret resistance force would meet them and the parts would be smuggled, piece by piece, into Berlin. There, it would be put together by Alfred's scientist and readied to do its job. Since the location was to be a secret basement in central Berlin, a timer was to be placed on it, so there would be time for all involved to get out before it worked."

"True, there were so many places where something could go wrong but they had to try. It was too important not to. For the very few involved, they were sure the incident would end all aggression and most likely prevent a war."

"Well, it was finally ready for shipment and the first ship available to take it was the Lusitania. Time was of the essence. Things were developing fast in Europe."

"Thinking about it now, I wonder if somehow, the plot got out and back to Germany. If it did, they would've known Alfred, the scientist and the device would be on the ship. They may have had some idea as to the power of the device and knew it had to be destroyed. The ship was the weakest link in the whole plan. That may be the reason it was necessary to sink the Lusitania."

Michael turned his head. "Okay, I know history and there was nothing around this time period that could have changed anything with the war. But of course, if it was THAT secret, it would never be known for the historical record. Do you know what this thing was?"

"All I know from talking with Alfred is it started with an element called uranium. And when it worked, it would be devastating. That material had been ready for some time and had been shipped to the forces there. It was the mechanism parts Alfred and his scientist were bringing over to the group."

Michael's jaw dropped. "You HAVE to be kidding! Oh, my God! Holy crap! You have to be kidding! It sounds like they had created… the atomic bomb!!"

"What?" Beatrice didn't understand, "What's an atomic bomb?"

"It is awesome. But it was not developed until the late nineteen-thirties." He looked at Jonathan. "You're telling me someone has already developed the atomic bomb?"

"Michael, this was so secret, not even the government knew of it. Governments move too slowly, so we in the financial and industrial community thought it was more important for us to try and figure out some way to stop the war as soon as possible. Alfred's scientist indicated it would most likely create a major explosion but as I said, it had never been tested. Everything was strictly theoretical. The scientist and Alfred were the only ones who knew how to assemble it. They were also the only ones who knew how to set it off. But no one was sure of its destructive capacity. The scientist was going to be smuggled aboard the Lusitania by Alfred and would stow away in his cabin. He was most likely hiding in an adjacent room while we were talking with Alfred."

"If what you are telling me is true, that scientist had discovered the most horrendous and devastating weapon ever developed by man. And, yes. It would have immediately had a deciding impact on whether there would've been a war. Believe it or not, with all its destructive capacity, the final assembly would not take up very much space. It wouldn't be that difficult for the resistance group to stay under the radar and get it into Berlin." Michael shook his head. "If this scientist didn't survive, it's most likely knowledge of the weapon would be lost until redeveloped later. Maybe someone found his papers years later if he saved anything like that."

"So, you know of this weapon? Under the radar? What is radar?"

"Radar hasn't been developed yet. I'll tell you about it sometime. And you will invest in it. It's going to be around and can make you some money." Then, Michael changed the subject, "The bomb. It didn't come to light until the beginning of the Second World War. It was used for the first time on Japan in nineteen forty-five."

"You mean there's going to be another war?" Jonathan cringed.

"Unfortunately, yes. A man named Hitler will come to power in Germany. It, too, is a conversation for another time."

"But what about the bomb? Would it have made a large explosion?"

"When it was used on the city of Hiroshima, it virtually leveled the city and killed over a hundred thousand people."

"It leveled the city!!? A hundred thousand people!!? Oh, my God! I had no idea of its power. That's astonishing!" Jonathan's face was one of shock and amazement.

"Astonishing!? It's terrifying!!" Beatrice expressed her displeasure.

Michael looked at Jonathan. "You just might be right. If Germany got wind of this and what it could do, they would've had a very good reason to want it destroyed along with the scientist who knew of its workings. And since Alfred was so intricately involved, he had no choice but to go with it. It all makes sense now. It has always been thought there were weapons on board the ship even though there were adamant denials of their existence. But no one knew there were the makings of an atomic bomb aboard. Holy crap! Damn!"

Jonathan grabbed at the middle of his upper chest. He could feel it under his shirt. "I guess Saint Christopher saved me."

"Saint Christopher and Michael." Beatrice replied.

Michael spoke up, "Saint Christopher, your Aunt Beatrice for believing me and especially Paul, Max's son, for showing me the newspaper, hanging on the wall in the office at Sandora. If that had not happened, I would NEVER have started this quest. 'There are more things in heaven and earth, Horatio, than are dreamt of in your philosophy.'"

"What?" Jonathan looked questioningly at Michael.

"I was just quoting the Bard. I thought it rather apropos to this whole situation. And another thing. It is not going to be pretty in Russia. There's going to be a major revolt and overthrow of the Czar. He and his immediate family will be killed in nineteen eighteen. So, if you have any relatives or investments there, I highly recommend they get out. Now!"

"Really? But the Romanov Family has been head of the country for some three hundred years. I can't imagine." Beatrice shook her head.

Michael tipped his head. "I know this may sound gruesome but after the overthrow, you can go in and buy extremely valuable things for a song. I heard that Lillian Pratt picked up a king's ransom in Fabergé eggs and jewelry, belonging to the Romanov family for next to nothing. She donated it all to the Virginia Museum of Fine Arts in Richmond in the late forties. Trust me. It's in the cards. And I know it more clearly than anyone else." He paused one moment, shaking his head, "And there's one more horror right around the corner. The Spanish Flu. It becomes prevalent in nineteen eighteen and kills millions of people. It will be essential for everyone to wear face masks and stay rather secluded till it wanes. Just a warning."

"I know that's right. And remember this. I will NEVER EVER doubt you again. I am sitting here because of you. Michael, I owe you my life. How will I ever repay you?" Jonathan was adamant.

"There is no pay." He looked lovingly at Jonathan. "For some reason, the Fates put me here in this time to meet you. And I believe, so I could save you. I cannot question it at this point." Michael was silent for a minute. "I just hope that if this changes history in a drastic manner, I truly hope it's for the good. I think because the Fates have been so kind to me to let me meet and come to know you, somehow, I'll be more understanding, aware of the suffering of others and do my best to help them."

"I definitely agree. With my money, we can make a huge difference. We must. You're right. And I say this now. My money is no longer just my money. It's now 'our' money. And shortly, I will have the legal documents drawn up to make it so." Jonathan slammed his fist in his palm. "Max and his family are very dear to me. If something were to ever happen to me, I want to make sure they are well taken care of. I will make sure the company that oversees the operations of Sandora and all its related properties are supported by the proper companies that I am associated with. I want large trusts established to take care of Max and his family in case something happens to me. I will get on this immediately."

Michael added, "Paul loves working at Sandora and most likely will continue to do so. But you are right. They need to know their future is secure. I like your ideas very much."

"Jonathan, I'd also like to start by doing something good for someone else. There's a young man I met along the way who was very helpful. He's ambitious and wants to go to college… university but doesn't have the means. I'd like to see about paying for his education and any expenses he has in getting his degree. I don't think you would be sorry. His name is Eric."

Jonathan nodded. "That's a wonderful idea. It's a new beginning and I think you're right. With the kind of money we'll be able to make because you know the future, it is only fitting we give back to help those in need and who deserve a helping hand. Consider it done."

"But he mustn't know where the money came from. There must be someone who will be in contact with him and know his expenses and pay them without him knowing the source. You know. Like in Great Expectations by Charles Dickens."

"Not a problem. I have many who can act as middlemen. And he will be the first of many."

Within the next month, a fund was set up for Eric, allowing him to get into college and study. After several years, he was on the fast track to becoming a prominent architect whose designs were in high demand. It pleased Michael to see Eric's career take off. In time, Michael saw several of Eric's creations and was truly impressed. He smiled in knowing he wasn't wrong about the ambitious young man he'd met those many years before.

It was 1956 in Eric's life when he heard Bill Haley and the Comets singing *See You Later, Alligator* that brought back a distant memory along with certain words that eventually started coming from the mouths of young people. That song and those words made him laugh as it took him back to when he was very young and heard them for the first time from a bearded man in a cowboy hat. Yes, every time he heard 'hip', 'cool' or 'groovy', he'd smile and remember that time long ago. *See You Later, Alligator* would forever be a very special song for him, too. One other thing that happened was his decision to go 'commando'. Ever since the time of meeting the cowboy back when he was young, he had tried it and totally agreed with what he'd said.

He also recalled a day in 1935. It was a Sunday. No one was on the premises that day and he was checking out the just completed architectural project he'd designed. It was a ten-story office complex.

The owners had spent a great deal of money to buy the entire city block even in that depression time in order to have a green space around it as well as a beautiful courtyard. The project was his crowning achievement, so far in his life. He thought it strange he never met the real owners. He always dealt with middlemen which did take some time to get ideas back and forth. But he didn't mind because the money was very good and he was given the freedom to put forth his design.

Passing one of the large windows on the fifth floor, he happened to look down and see a big car pull up to the edge of the property. Looking closer, he realized it was a 1934 Rolls-Royce limousine. He stood peering out the window to see just who it might be. The driver got out of the car and opened the back door. Out stepped a tall, distinguished man with coal-black hair, beard and mustache, dressed in a tailored dark vested suit and top hat. He also noticed the man was wearing a black eye patch.

"Dressed like that, I'll bet he's some banker." He spoke quietly to himself.

Then, out stepped a shorter man with white hair, beard and mustache, dressed in tan pants, tan jacket, brown boots and a brown cowboy hat. Watching this man, Eric realized the shorter man was explaining something to the tall man. The way the shorter man was waving his arms would have been the same gestures he would have used to call attention to details of the architecture.

"That man has to have an architectural background. I wonder who they are?" He spoke softly. His mind whirled. Suddenly, it came to him. "I'll bet they're the owners."

The sunlight glinted off the gold of the hatband and instantly, Eric was back, a young man in Richmond. It was the day a guest at the hotel arrived, dressed in cowboy attire. He also accompanied him shopping the next day. They'd stopped at a small restaurant for coffee and they talked. "Michael. Yes. His name was Michael. Mister Michael." Eric smiled. He remembered him being very determined, yet gracious. Michael had told him to always go with his gut, his dreams. Regardless of how difficult or far afield it may seem. It's Destiny calling you. Even if things get in your way, don't give up. That had constantly stuck with him throughout his life and had made him the man he was.

Eric could feel, from their conversation in that restaurant, that Michael was on some difficult mission and it had to be completed no matter the consequences or outcome. He wondered what had happened to him and if he found his Destiny. "I hope he is well and happy."

Popping back to reality again, Eric watched the two men. Finally, the shorter man stopped his gestures. Eric could see a huge smile on his face. Somehow, that face and smile seemed familiar. It was the smile of approval and being proud. Then, the short man raised his arms and clapped his hands in applause. A thought like a bolt of lightning hit him. "Could it be him? After all these years? Could it be him?"

Suddenly, he heard a distant voice in his head, "I will make sure you are the first one I call for. You never know. I may need a good architect one of these days down the road." They'd been spoken by Mister Michael those many years earlier in Richmond. Excitement raced through his body. But before there was time to get down to them, Eric saw them head back to the car, get in and drive off. He stood there in silence. Somehow, in his heart, he felt and knew it was his kind and generous cowboy from the past. A big smile filled his face.

He was absolutely correct and the complex was for one of Jonathan's organizations. Michael had insisted Eric be the architect and have free rein on the design, regardless of cost. And, so it was.

Not long after the complex opened, Eric received a letter.

Dear Eric,

You may not remember me after all this time but I have watched your progress and success over the years. I am very proud of you for sticking to your guns, regarding your dreams and your designs. I have seen several of your works and each and every one made me smile with delight at its beauty and style. I once said to you that I might need a good architect one day. Well, you are not a good architect, you are a great and incredibly talented one. I shall continue to follow your work as long as I live. Mark my words. They will be remembering you in the architectural world even after another 200 years or more.

Jonathan and I wanted you to be the one to do the complex for one of Jonathan's companies. This complex you designed for us is an added example of your amazing talent. Thank you for doing it for us.

And just so you will know. Do you remember I told you I was on a very difficult quest? Well, I wanted you to know, I accomplished it and everything has turned out exceedingly well.

I want to thank you again for your help back in Richmond, those so many years ago. You were very kind and thoughtful. Take care, my friend, be happy and keep up the good work. It is totally.... COOL!!!!

Respectfully yours,
Michael Groves

After reading the letter, he began to laugh at the last word. He was so happy as he'd thought of Michael many times over the years. Matted and framed, the letter hung in his office or home, keeping it near throughout his life. Seeing it always made him happy.

He had several times contemplated going and meeting both Michael and Jonathan but realized they wanted their anonymity. He wanted to respect their desire.

—◦◦◦◦—

Jonathan turned to Michael. "Now, I must tell you everything." He looked at Beatrice, who smiled and nodded her approval. He looked back at Michael. "I've told you much of my history and all I told you was true. But it was not the whole truth. I'm going to tell you the secret only Aunt Beatrice and I know. No one else can know it, at least not right now. It has to do with my wealth."

Michael's face took on a very concerned look, "Oh, NO!" Michael yelled out, "You're broke! Something happened and you lost all your money! Oh, Jonathan. I'm sorry. I'm so sorry. But it's okay. I never had any. So, don't worry. We'll still make it. And we'll take care of Aunt Beatrice. Jonathan, I still love you. I don't care about your money. I'll stop painting and go to work."

Jonathan looked at Beatrice with a huge grin, "I can't believe how so right you are about him." He nodded his head. "You truly called it." He looked back at Michael. "Okay. It's time for more coffee all around before I start to tell you how broke I am." He got up and prepared a cup for all three, then returned to his seat and began.

"Michael. No. I have not gone broke. Actually, quite the contrary. But let me explain. When my father died, his estate was divided as everyone knows. But what everyone doesn't know is about the large envelope he had given me for safekeeping, telling me it was not to be opened until his death. No one knew of its existence, except me and Aunt Beatrice, of course."

"When I opened it, there were two letters. The first letter was to let me know he was, in actuality, my real father as stated in his will and how proud he was of me. The second letter told me no one was to ever know of the rest of the envelope's contents or its significance. There was information and proof that, yes, my father was rich and had a substantial estate. The estate that was divided at his death. But in actuality, he was worth a great deal more. A GREAT deal more. All hidden in banks around the world and in business ties under many names that were virtually untraceable to him. The documents enclosed would prove I would be the beneficiary upon his death and would assume his place. So. What I'm trying to say is, there is no worry about money."

Beatrice spoke up, "If it were known, Jonathan could buy and sell everyone he knows. Yes. All his wealthy friends and associates. None of them have any idea as to how wealthy he really is. It would be fair to say, Jonathan is the richest man in the world. He is worth several billion dollars. But the way it is so convoluted, it would be virtually impossible to connect the dots to Jonathan."

Michael's mouth hung open. "You HAVE to be kidding me! Really!? Really!? It sounds like you are telling me you have more money than God!"

Jonathan laughed, "Well, that might be one way of putting it."

They all looked at one another and broke into loud laughter.

"Well, let me warn you. There is coming a thing called 'income tax'. Yeah. Not long from now. So, you better make sure your assets are well documented and you can prove a lot of deductions. If you don't, a huge amount of your money will end up in the government's pocket, not yours. Trust me. I filed mine several weeks ago. Ah, in nineteen eighty-two. And the way the government WASTES money, irks me to no end."

"Thanks for the warning. I'll definitely have the accountants check into it."

"I think this calls for something a lot more than coffee." Beatrice went to the phone, calling down to the dining room. After a few moments, she returned and sat down.

Soon, there was a knock at the door. A young man was pushing a small cart with three urns filled with ice and a bottle of champagne in each. "Mister Jonathan, I'm sure you are celebrating your decision to not leave for England last Saturday. The Fates must be watching over you. I'm so glad you are still with us. Gerald, at the front desk, wanted you to know that all the staff and management want to express their gladness of you cheating the Grim Reaper. Again. He was glad that Mister Michael accomplished getting you off the ship. We are so sorry to hear about your friend, Mister Alfred." He rolled the cart into the room near where they were all sitting.

Jonathan walked him back to the door and handed him a gratuity. "Thank you, Robert. We appreciate it. Tell everyone I thank them for their kind words. Yes, I tried to get Alfred to leave the ship but he was insistent that he needed to go on the trip. It is sad."

"You are so welcome, Mister Jonathan." He bowed slightly, turned and left.

Jonathan returned to the sitting area. Beatrice had been to her cabinet and obtained three crystal goblets. After the telltale 'pop', Jonathan poured each glass then placed the bottle back in the urn. He took his glass and remained standing. He raised his glass.

Beatrice and Michael stood and raised their glasses.

Jonathan looked into Michael's eyes. "What can I say? I do love you and I promise you I will try to make you happy. I hope you will become as proud of me as Aunt Beatrice is. I'm going to see you never want for anything. If you need it, let me know. It's yours."

Michael looked back at Jonathan. "I already have all that is important to me. You. Everything else is icing on the cake." He turned to Beatrice. "Aunt Beatrice. Thank you so much for your faith and belief in me. I will always love you for it. I will try to always make you proud of me just as you are of Jonathan. Well. Not about money. I can never make as much money as Jonathan but maybe for some other reason." He sheepishly bent his head down.

"My dears. My boys." Beatrice spoke softly, "I am already more proud of both of you than you could ever imagine. Nothing could make me more proud of you than I am right now. Seeing you both together and how you care about one another makes me very happy and proud. Trust me. Both of you, together, are going to make your mark on the world whether others realize it or not. I will know. And know I love you both." She set her glass down and walked over to each, caressing their faces with both hands and kissing them on their lips. She returned to her place and picked up her glass again.

Their glasses rang as they touched. It truly was a new beginning for all of them.

CHAPTER XX

Paul walked slowly to the pavilion. He could not keep up with Michael who was way ahead of him. Arriving at the iron gate in the stone wall, he saw it was chained shut. It was obvious no one had been there in a very long time. He looked around and called out, "Mister Michael! Mister Michael!" There was no response. "Where could he have gone?" He muttered. He yelled out again, "Mister Michael! Mister Michael!" Still nothing. He shook his head. After a few minutes, he headed back to the hotel.

Arriving back at the front desk, Martin looked at him. "Where's Mister Michael? He ran out of here like he was shot out of a cannon, yelling out. What was that all about, 'saving yesterday'? It makes no sense and he really looked intense."

"I have no idea. I couldn't find him. Maybe he will return."

"Did he go crazy? Should we call someone?"

"No. I think he's out there, trying to find himself. I think he'll be all right. He'll be back." Paul was so disturbed in wondering if Michael could actually get back there and have an influence on the past. He knew he would have to keep it a secret. No one would ever believe him if he tried to tell them that he thought Michael had gone back in time to 1915.

Two days passed and there was no sign of Michael. Paul finally became very concerned. He wasn't sure what to do. He called the local police and explained that one of the guests had run out of the hotel in a very distraught state and hadn't been seen since. There was no way he would tell them that he believed Michael had gone back in time. Anyone hearing that would think he was having a mental issue. He had to keep that information to himself.

The officer was pleasant and indicated that yes, he had done the right thing and he'd have someone check into it.

On Thursday morning, there was still no sign of Michael, so Paul had all of his things from his rooms packed up and brought to the pavilion and placed in the guest bedroom there. "Michael's things should be with Jonathan's." He'd go and sort it at a later time. He had Michael's car put in the employee parking lot for safekeeping till things were settled.

Saturday, May 8th, arrived. Paul was in the main office, sitting at the desk. He happened to glance up at the framed newspaper, hanging on the wall. The date was clear. It was from Saturday, May 8th, 1915. The bold black headlines had faded some but he could read them clearly. 'JONATHAN WOLFE DROWNS IN LUSITANIA SINKING!' There was a picture of the Lusitania and a formal picture of Jonathan. The script went on to read. 'Yesterday, the man who cheated the Grim Reaper three years ago by not making it to the Titanic before it sailed, did not escape this time.'

Paul lowered his head. "What a shame. Sixty-seven years ago, yesterday, May the seventh." He spoke very softly, "I could tell how much Mister Michael cared for him." He shook his head and felt very sad. He whispered a silent prayer for them both.

His moment of respect over, he raised his head. Out of the corner of his eyes, he saw the newspaper again. Suddenly, it hit him. He turned quickly and stood up. He stared right at the paper and gasped in amazement. The date was the same but he read the headlines out loud, "'JONATHAN WOLFE CHEATS DEATH FROM THE SEA A SECOND TIME!'" Paul kept reading, "'Yesterday, Mister Jonathan Wolfe escaped death from drowning at sea again! A business meeting prevented him from making passage on the Titanic the first time. This time, a good friend convinced him to leave the Lusitania last Saturday, just before it set sail from New York. He has to be charmed with luck!'"

Paul grabbed his heart. He began to laugh and cry at the same time. He limped out of the office, yelling out, "He made it! He made it! Somehow, he did it!" He thought for a moment, "I understand, now. He did just what he said he was trying to do by... saving yesterday." He began to think about it. Everything he remembered from the past was correct and Jonathan would have died even though Michael had been in the past prior to May 7th. But Michael made it back and changed history significantly by saving Jonathan. From the moment Jonathan was saved, history from that point on was changed to the present, starting on May 7th but it took until now for the shock wave of the change to reach here. Even though he appeared upset, he was actually incredibly happy and pleased.

Martin happened to be standing behind the desk and saw how Paul was acting. "Paul! Are you all right!? Why are you laughing and crying at the same time?"

"He made it! Michael made it! I'm so happy for them. He made it."

"Paul! Here! Come with me and sit down." Martin led him to the sitting area near the fireplace. The same place Paul had his talk with Michael days earlier. "Let me get you some hot tea."

Paul sat there for a moment, thinking about all Michael had told him. Then, suddenly, his whole body shook and his leg twitched.

Instantly, a distant memory flashed into his mind. It was August 24th, 1920. He was out in the front of the hotel playing when the ball he was playing with went out into the parking lot. Just as he was getting ready to run after it, a hand grabbed him and held him with a firm grip just as a car went by. He realized if it hadn't been for the hand holding him back, the car would have hit him. When he turned, he looked up into the smiling face of a bearded man, wearing a cowboy hat. It was the same hat that had been placed on his head years earlier in the dining room. He remembered the man speaking.

"It's August twenty-fourth. I knew I had to be… right here. I owed it to you for all you have done for me. If not for you, I would not be standing here at this moment." Then, he smiled, "Paul. You will be all right now. You may not understand what I have just said. But you will reflect on it in years to come. Then, it will make sense to you."

Paul smiled in the reverie. He remembered it clearly. He knew the man. "Mister Michael. And he was with Mister Jonathan." At that instant, he knew something had happened to him physically. He stood up and took a few steps. His leg was no longer crippled. Tears rolled down his face. "Mister Michael saved my leg!" He realized if Michael had not made it back, this never would have happened.

Martin returned with a tray and placed it on the table. "Here, Paul. Let me fix you a cup. You look like you could use it."

Paul giggled, "I think I could use more than hot tea." He began to laugh.

"Paul, what is it? What is going on? Is there anything I can do?" He looked at Paul's leg. "Is your leg all right?"

"Oh, Martin. I am fine now. I understand. Everything is all

right. Yes, everything IS all right." He couldn't remove the huge smile or stop the tears from streaming down his face.

"Okay. If you say so." Martin returned to the front desk.

Paul slowly got up to test out his leg by walking slowly around the area. He was out about fifteen feet from the fireplace when he saw something that hadn't been there before. It was a large painting above the mantel in a wide gold leaf frame. He looked at it and began to smile and tears filled his eyes again.

It was a life-size painting of a man in western attire, sitting in a chair, a cowboy hat in his lap and a man with a patch over his left eye, wearing black formal attire, a black silk top hat held in his left hand, standing beside and slightly behind him, his right hand resting on the seated man's left shoulder. Both men had big smiles on their faces, their teeth showing. The seated man's brown eyes seemed to sparkle with glee. The intense green eye of the standing man seemed to look into your soul. The painting was of such detail, it was like the two men could step right out of it. Paul looked over the whole picture. Down in the lower right-hand corner was a small banner. He looked closely at it. There was something written on it. He looked closer. He began to giggle.

Paul softly read the words aloud, "'We made it, Paul. And no, I did not do this painting. The great Mister Sargent did.'" He looked at the other corner and saw the artist's signature and date. He smiled and looked back up at the painting and Jonathan's hand on Michael's shoulder, "Mister Michael was always Mister Jonathan's 'right-hand man'."

Pieces of memories began to flood in and unfold in his head. He began to remember many incidences of seeing Michael and Jonathan together over the years.

Then, he remembered the day construction started on a gallery Jonathan was building for Michael. He walked out the front door and onto the front veranda. There it was, a wonderful addition to the hotel complex, down near the terrace of the dining room. He smiled, realizing yesterday nothing was there, and yet, it had been there for years.

Over the next week, Paul took the time to go through the gallery. It was like seeing the paintings there and hearing the piano music for the first time. He also visited the chapel and brought red roses for everyone lying there. It was virtually calming to see all the names and know he would eventually be joining them. It was comforting to know he would be with the ones he cared for and loved in life.

Paul had grown up in the shadow and world of Sandora and the people around it. But his life was exactly as he wanted it. Everyone was so concerned because he never married but he'd had several relationships, lasting for several years. All ended with everyone remaining good friends. He knew he was not the marrying kind and let it be known from the start. He loved his single life and had no regrets about the matter.

His parents were of the few in on the secret that Michael was from the future and was part of their ability to invest and make great sums of money. Although quite wealthy, they were of the same thinking as Jonathan. One needs to work to keep in touch with humanity. Max could not imagine doing anything other than being a chef. He loved it. To him, it wasn't like work at all.

Even after his extensive education, travels and his many interests, Paul stayed working at Sandora. It was his choice. He loved it since the work was mostly laid-back and he loved the people he'd meet from around the world. Many were return visitors, again and again. His own travels gave him an insight into many cultures and ways of life.

And when it was his time, he told many how full and wonderful his life had been and he would not have changed a thing nor had it any other way. He was happy in the knowledge his final resting place would be next to his parents and would be the last to be laid to rest in the chapel.

Yes, Jonathan and Michael shared an incredible and rewarding life together. Beatrice treated Michael like another son. She always referred to them as 'her boys'. It became obvious from the start that Michael was destined to stay in Jonathan's time. He thought it a small price to pay and he constantly told Jonathan he would never have had it any other way. One thing the small select group realized was no one could know Michael was from the future and they'd have to keep it secret. They didn't need anyone looking into their lives with a magnifying glass.

Over the years, they visited many museums and went all over the world. One of the great things they were proud of was the help they provided for many where they saw the need, by giving anonymous gifts. Michael always said it was a small price to pay for the great sums of money they made in knowing the future and investing wisely. And all their donations were tax-deductible. This made Michael very happy.

Virtually, from the first months they were together, Michael pushed Jonathan to practice his piano. Eventually, he became quite proficient. Many said he was concert quality but Jonathan only played at parties and private functions. His favorite thing was to play for a charitable event and raise money for a good cause. When they were invited to events, it was known Jonathan would play several pieces and everyone looked forward to it. Every time they were invited to a party, beforehand, Michael would get with Jonathan to pick out a few pieces to learn. Michael was so proud of Jonathan and the praise he got for his incredible playing. For once in his life, he was getting praise for his unquestionable talent and not his money. This made Michael very happy. And he could see the joy on Jonathan's face with the adulations.

During the times Jonathan would be practicing, Michael would have his easel set up and paint while listening to Jonathan's playing.

Michael's paintings were exceptional. Jonathan was so pleased with Michael's work, he built a small gallery near the hotel just off the terrace of the dining room. It maintained the same style as the hotel but having no windows, just two doors, one at each end. A large skylight was installed in the roof to light the interior. The exterior walls were accented with ornate Gothic niches, holding statuary to break the blank surfaces.

The gallery was for the display of Michael's work and the paintings that originally belonged to Aunt Beatrice after she passed away. His paintings were for sale. There was a rotating show of twenty-five of his paintings. The one painting that was the focal point of the room was the one Michael had done of Jonathan's pavilion. The one he'd given him when first they met. Michael finally got around to signing and dating it. Yes. He put 1982 with 1915 right under it as the date. This painting was never to be sold. Jonathan loved it and wanted everyone who came to see it. Many were curious when they saw the dates. You could see it on their faces. But no one ever questioned it. Of course, the sale of Michael's paintings would end with his death. The paintings that were in the gallery at that time would remain in the gallery for all time.

As the state of the art of music reproduction got better and better, Michael had professional recordings made of a very long list of pieces played by Jonathan, placed on a rotating continuous play in the gallery when it was open. To Michael, it was just another way they would share the same place and space with their individual talents. This would be updated when newer forms of recording became available. This prevented the earlier forms of records and reel-to-reel recording tapes from deteriorating in quality. Also, multiple copies would be made just in case some accident damaged or destroyed a copy.

From the beginning, Michael encouraged Jonathan to work on many of the pieces written by one of his contemporaries, "Jonathan, there is someone alive right now who will become one of Twentieth Century's greatest composers for the piano. His music is incredible. I have a sneaking suspicion you already know who I'm talking about"

Jonathan looked up in the air with his mouth open, "Aahhhhh. Did he write a piece called, *Prelude in C-Sharp Minor?*" He looked at Michael with a huge grin.

"Yes, you silly goose. And wait till you hear the piece he will write in nineteen thirty-four. It's one of the most beautiful pieces of piano music. It's one of my favorites."

"Nineteen thirty-four? So, I have to wait twelve years?"

"Correct. It will be called the *Eighteenth Variation* from the *Rhapsody on a Theme of Paganini*. Yep. Long name for such a short piece. But just wait. It is, ah, will be written for piano and orchestra and the composition has twenty-four variations. Absolutely incredible. Big huge chords all over the piano. You're going to love it." Michael gave a big grin, "It was transcribed for piano only because it is… will be, so beautiful and everyone will want to play it. Now, you know I could plunk it out for you."

"All right. I'm ready. Let's hear it." Jonathan loved it when Michael would do these things of pulling something from the future for him to know, before its time.

Michael walked over to the piano bench and made Jonathan scoot over. So, he began. As he played the piece in a fair manner, Jonathan closed his eyes to capture the total essence of it all. Finally, the last chords faded into the air and they both sat silent for a few moments.

Jonathan opened his eyes and took a breath, "Damn. That is incredibly beautiful."

"Wait till you hear all those big chords played well like you will do when you do it twelve years from now. It can bring tears to your eyes. But, yes, you have to wait another twelve years." He gave another big grin.

Another question Jonathan had that Michael got the chance to answer was regarding the painting of the portrait. Jonathan wanted the portrait done and wondered if Michael knew of a good artist since he didn't do them. Michael was well aware of one of the most famous portrait painters living during this time. So, in 1920, they went to London, England and contacted John Singer Sargent, commissioning him to do not just Jonathan's portrait but the portrait of both Michael and Jonathan together.

They found it very interesting when Sargent said that he had done a portrait of two men back in 1912. A Mister Andrew

Cavenaugh and a Mister Brian Durnam from New York. He was quite pleased how that painting turned out. They were going to hang it in the great room of their house that was being built on an island off the coast of Maine.

Looking at Jonathan closely, Sargent asked if it was possible he was related to Andrew Cavenaugh as the resemblance was uncanny. He indicated that Jonathan and Andrew looked like they could be brothers. Jonathan had no idea but told John that he would look into it. One never knows.

Mister Sargent was confused but amused at the banner and message Michael wanted in the lower right-hand corner of their painting. When completed and dry, it was shipped to the United States. Jonathan got with some people at the Metropolitan Museum of Art in New York to have them frame it for him. This was not a problem. When it was done, it was shipped to Sandora and was hung in the lobby above the main fireplace.

Because of the comments made by Sargent, Jonathan was curious and did some investigating. He did find some information regarding Andrew Cavenaugh. Andrew left his apartment in New York in the spring of 1919 and moved to a house out on an island off the coast of Maine. Jonathan also found out there was a strange backstory about a failed relationship. His bride-to-be was marrying him only for his money and was going to have him killed soon after their marriage, so she could inherit all his wealth. Obviously, the marriage never took place. Not long after moving to the house, he disappeared. No one ever saw or heard from him again. There was virtually no information on Andrew that could provide any indications of a possible relationship with Jonathan.

For some reason, Jonathan just couldn't let it go. His curiosity was so great that he and Michael took a trip up to Maine after Jonathan found out exactly where the house and island were located. One of Jonathan's clients offered to take them up on his boat and they sailed right to the island. Jonathan wanted to see if the painting of Andrew was still in the house and if he really did resemble Andrew.

They were surprised that they were able to get in the house and look around. It was still not completely finished construction-wise and empty of any furniture or belongings. It was a total dead end. Jonathan was disappointed but Michael convinced him that it was not a wasted trip since it basically closed the door on that question.

Over the years, this subject would occasionally come up in conversation as it always seemed to be somewhere in the back of Jonathan's mind. It was something that would continue to be a mystery to them.

It was like a wonderful dream. They lived their lives with love and adventure. No place in the world was out of their reach.

Beatrice passed away in 1926 the same year as Monet. She was brought to the chapel and buried next to her brother, Jonathan's actual father. Jonathan was so happy Michael was there for him to console him. Aunt Beatrice had been so loving and caring. He knew his own mother couldn't have loved him more.

Michael discovered the chapel truly was Jonathan's special place since it was the resting place of all those Jonathan loved in life. All were buried in the floor of the chapel in stone vaults and covered with large stone slabs. Bronze plaques were embedded in the walls with the names, dates and commemorative sayings on them. Even several of the stained glass windows were tributes to those interred there.

Long before October of 1929, Michael had already warned Jonathan of the financial crash that would take place, allowing Jonathan to take the proper precautions to avoid a catastrophe in the finances of those around him.

Over the years, Michael would tell Jonathan about certain upcoming events or inventions, allowing Jonathan to invest wisely. Michael told him not to be greedy as he did have an unfair advantage over everyone else. Jonathan thought it wise and took his advice and major profits were given to deserving charities. It was interesting because in several cases, the companies involved were actually part of Jonathan's wealth in those convoluted holdings.

One other thing Jonathan was adamant about. He was alive because of all the events surrounding Michael coming to the hotel. They made a reservation far in the future for Michael at Sandora for a two-week stay, starting on Wednesday, April 7th, 1982, knowing that's when he would be coming. Michael recalled the day he first arrived at the hotel and found his reservations were already paid for and never knew who did it. Now, he knew and it made him laugh that HE actually was influential in making his own reservations and paying for it many years in advance. That's why the card and note looked so old that day.

Then, there were the numbers, four-o-seven. Michael and Jonathan both believed it was the Fates letting Michael know he was on the right path, leading him to Jonathan.

As the years passed, they both stayed in good physical health, not gaining weight or seeming to age. Many thought it was because they were always so happy. Jonathan's hair, mustache and beard would forever remain black as onyx. Michael's dark brown hair, mustache and beard eventually turned snow-white but it never made him look old. It actually accented his dark brown eyes. Everyone loved them, saying they always looked like such a handsome distinguished pair.

It was in June of 1965. Michael went down and got coffee for them both. When he returned, Jonathan was still in bed. "Jonathan, I have your coffee. Now, don't forget. Max is coming down from the hotel to talk with you this morning about upcoming events but not for a while yet."

Jonathan looked up from his bed. "I know. Max has some great ideas for the Fourth." He paused for a moment, "You know. My arm hurts. It just feels funny." He reached over with his right arm and rubbed his left one.

"Here, let me hold you." Michael put the tray down on the dresser and went over, propped up several pillows against the headboard of the bed then got in. "Lean forward, so I can get in behind you." He crawled in, put one leg on either side of Jonathan then leaned back against the pillows. "Now, scoot back and lay back." Jonathan moved back between Michael's legs, resting on Michael's chest, his head up near Michael's left shoulder. Michael brushed back Jonathan's coal-black hair with his right hand then rubbed Jonathan's chest and arms and kissed the top of his head. "Does that feel better?"

"Yes, it does. You're too good to me. Thank you." Jonathan was silent for a moment, enjoying Michael's caring touch. Then, he spoke softly, "Thank you. Thank you so much."

"Oh, Jonathan. Don't be silly. It's nothing. Just as long as you're feeling better."

"No. Seriously. I mean for everything. I can't believe how lucky and fortunate I am and have been." A big smile covered his face, "Do you know? I can close my eyes and I can still see you that first time? That handsome cowboy, crossing the dining room and sitting next to the windows. Wow! Yes. You know to me, you're still so handsome. I have to admit, my first thoughts back then were strictly physical when I invited you here to the cottage that night. But when you did show up and we began to talk, I was totally taken aback. The things you were interested in and in doing were so incredible. And as we talked through that first week, I came to know a man who was caring and giving, not expecting anything in return. And then, you gave me the painting of the cottage. What can I say? I finally knew God had been so kind to me to give me the chance to meet you and I knew you were the one I wanted to share my life with." He paused for a moment, "Do you know I was so afraid you might not like me?" He snickered.

"Through the years, I have never known a more wonderful man and I know I haven't told you enough how much I care for and love you. You have given me so much happiness. I wish others could have just a small portion of the kind of happiness I've had with and because of you. You've always been so supportive of everything I've done and you've given me direction on things of which to beware." He patted the top of Michael's hand. "Do you know how much I have loved how you dote on me? You always seem to know what I need or want before I do. And you never seem to be bothered with it."

He squeezed Michael's hand and pulled it over his heart, pressing it down on his chest. "But most of all, for saving my life. If not for you, I would have died on May the seventh way back then and I'd have missed it all. And you gave up your own life in your time to stay with me. Michael. What can I say? Please, know how much I appreciate you and love you. I love you so much. You have made my life more than I could have ever imagined." He squeezed Michael's hand again. "I hope I have given you at least half of what you have given me."

Michael spoke quietly, "It is you who has made my life the best I could have ever thought it could be. They say actions speak louder than words. And all the things you have done. I can't tell you the joy and the pleasure you've given me. I, too, have wished everyone could be so lucky to have such a great life with such a wonderful, caring and loving person." He gave a little chuckle, "Funny you should mention that first night in the dining room. I can see it clear as day in my mind as if it were yesterday. I had never seen such a handsome man in all my life. You're as handsome now as you were then. I was absolutely floored when you sent me that note inviting me here." He paused for a moment, "And as far as doting on you. I have loved doing things for you if I knew it made you happy or would make you smile. Seeing a glint of joy on your face always brings such a feeling that goes through me. It makes me feel so good." He kissed the top of Jonathan's head. "Jonathan… I love you more than words can say. My heart is happy because of you. Because of you, my life has been full and incredibly amazing. I love you so much. Thank you for ALL you have given me." There was a moment of silence and he kissed the top of Jonathan's head again. "Would you like a cup of coffee now? I'll get it for you."

"No. Not yet. I like you just holding me and being here with me. Is that all right?" He pulled Michael's hand up to his mouth and kissed it then placed it back on his chest.

"Of course, silly. I like holding you." Michael and Jonathan lay together, Michael slightly rocking back and forth, still rubbing Jonathan's chest and arms and periodically kissing the top of Jonathan's head. Jonathan kept holding Michael's hand and periodically squeezing it.

After a while, Michael noticed Jonathan wasn't squeezing his hand any longer. "Jonathan?" He spoke softly. He smiled for a moment. Jonathan must have fallen asleep again. He leaned his head over and kissed the top of Jonathan's head. Then, suddenly, he became aware Jonathan's chest was not moving. Michael stopped rocking and was silent for a while. He immediately realized. He knew.

His head tilted back. He closed his eyes. He bit down on his lower lip with his top teeth and began to softly cry. Tears ran down his cheeks and disappeared into his snow-white beard. He kept holding Jonathan and began slowly rocking back and forth again and whispered, "Jonathan… I love you. I love you so much. I love you beyond death. I love you forever."

After a while, he kissed the top of Jonathan's head again. He lay still and then quietly, slowly and calmly he spoke,

> "'And when he shall die,
> Take him and cut him out in little stars,
> And he shall make the face of heaven so fine
> That all in the world will be in love with night
> And pay no worship to the garish sun.'"

"Goodnight, my love. Goodnight, my life."

He lay there quietly and kissed the top of Jonathan's head one last time. Then, after a moment of silence, he leaned his head over on top of Jonathan's and began to softly sing, "'Some enchanted evening... you will see a stranger... You will see a stranger... across a crowded room...'"

By mid-morning on that same day, Max came down with breakfast. The Fourth of July celebration would be coming up in less than a month and he wanted to cover a few things about it with Jonathan. When he entered the pavilion, he called out for Jonathan but there was no answer. He called out for Michael but there was no answer. He placed the food and dishes on the bar cabinet. He thought it strange. He was sure they would be up by then. Jonathan had called the night before and asked for breakfast to be brought down to the pavilion at this time.

Max walked all around. They were not there, so he went upstairs and called again. There was no response. He went to Michael's room and knocked on the door. There was no answer. "Mister Michael? It's Max." There was no answer. Max opened the door. Michael was not there. He went to Jonathan's room and knocked. "Mister Jonathan? It's Max. I brought breakfast." There was no answer. Max opened the door and looked in.

There on Jonathan's bed was Michael, propped up on the pillows, still holding Jonathan against his chest, his head leaning over on the top of Jonathan's. "Mister Michael?" He spoke quietly, "Mister Jonathan?"

For a moment, Max was totally confused. He wasn't sure if they were asleep. But then he realized. He knew. He slowly went over and looked closer.

Jonathan's face was one of peace and serenity, a soft smile on it. Michael's face was still wet from tears he had shed. They both were gone. Max could tell Jonathan died first and happy in Michael's arms. There was a smile on Michael's face as well, knowing he was following right behind Jonathan. They were together.

He stood there, silent. Tears began to run down his face for the loss of his two dearest friends but also with a touch of joy, knowing they were in death just as they were in life... together.

Yes. Michael's prophetic words came true. He had said he couldn't live without Jonathan. And, so it was. Many said Michael's heart broke but being with Jonathan and holding him in his final moments, gave him the happiness to smile as he joined Jonathan. Just like the words of the song. He 'never let him go'.

The ceremony for them both was not elaborate or flashy. The service inside the chapel was only for very, very close friends. Outside the doors and around the chapel were hundreds who came to pay their respect, those who knew of their help and service. Speakers were set up, so they could hear the service.

Jonathan and Michael were cremated and their ashes placed in one single urn. It was buried in the chapel under a single stone slab in the floor in front of the shrine to Saint Christopher.

There was one man who heard and came to show his respect. He was even permitted to speak when Max realized who he was. As he spoke, he revealed his story and how he had discovered who his benefactors were, allowing him to obtain a fine education and become the man he was. He never got to thank them in life, knowing they wanted their anonymity but he felt it only fitting he should be present as they left it. Eric said he never got to meet Jonathan in person but he remembered with great fondness his encounter with the man he would always call Mister Michael. He was so honored to have had such men influence his life.

Paul was always amused when he would go to visit the chapel and see the bronze plaques, containing the names and dates for Jonathan and Michael. They had a patina over their entire surface, except for the date of Michael's birth. '1946'. These numbers were well polished from fingers rubbing over their surface. Yes, people would see them with a question on their faces and had to touch them to make sure their eyes hadn't deceived them, thinking full well there had to be some big mistake. But the touching, only proved their eyes had seen the numbers correctly. Then, a much larger question mark would fill their facial expression. He would chuckle to himself, watching them, knowing their minds were clicking and whirling, trying to understand the calculation and putting it to reality. They would shake their heads and leave more perplexed than when they arrived. Only Max, his wife and Paul knew the secret. The date was absolutely... correct.

There was one other major historical catastrophe that should be mentioned before this story is completely over. Michael's knowledge of the future made him step in to save the day... once again. It was in May of 1937. He and Jonathan had been touring in Europe, celebrating the year of Jonathan's sixtieth birthday. They were returning to the States before embarking on another trip in early summer.

For years afterward, Jonathan loved to retell the story at parties, acting out the moment, knowing it got a nice shock effect at the end, especially after everyone knew the possible consequences of the event. Yes, Jonathan and Michael knew the real truth but for everyone else, it seemed another immense stroke of luck, especially after Michael had prevented Jonathan from going down on the Lusitania.

After several cocktails had been served all around, Jonathan would stand up and start, "Yes, we were coming home and I told Michael I had made reservations on a leisure trip back to the States from Frankfurt. We would be landing in New Jersey on May the sixth. I thought it would be a great way to come back. Of course, I made no mention as to how we would be traveling." That's when he'd look over to Michael. "Okay. Now, you can tell them what you said." He'd shake his head, grin and flex his eyebrows.

Michael always seemed reluctant to do the act but knew there was no getting out of it. So, he would stand up and do the part. In a slow and determined voice, he would speak with a pensive look on his face, "And how are we to get home from Frankfurt?" At this point, there would be a very long pause as he would always look out at everyone watching and shaking his head. Then, his face would take on a look similar to the famous deadpan, Jack Benny expression. He'd look up into the air as if he'd had some revelation then look back at Jonathan again and slowly and deliberately speak his final lines, "Frankfurt to New Jersey? Wow! Landing on May the sixth? Really? Landing? Landing?" He'd look around the room at everyone again with a big Cheshire Cat grin on his face then speak very deliberately and quietly as he turned in Jonathan's direction, "Jonathan. What would you think of doing this instead? How about you cancel the reservations you made and let's take a train to Paris, then Cherbourg and take the next ship to New York? We're in no hurry and that would be a nice leisurely trip. Hey! That way we just might get to go home on the Queen Mary... and NOT... on the Hindenburg!"

The End

Printed in the United States
by Baker & Taylor Publisher Services